The Perfect

Relationship

HOW IMPERFECT PEOPLE CAN CREATE A PERFECT
RELATIONSHIP

DR. CAROLYN WHITE-BROWN

D1530599

Dedication

A few years ago, I was talking to my best friend Claudette about relationships, things that women go through with the men in their lives. I found myself going back to the problems I had before I met the man of my dreams, the man I have been married to for over forty years. After thinking about the few bad relationships, I had gone through, and now being happily married, I thought it would be a great idea to write a book about relationships, both bad and good.

Thanks to my sons, Allen and Todd who are such great sons, husbands and fathers and supported me from day one on this project, to my sisters, Doris and Evelyn, and my daughter, Carol who helped me immensely. What a pleasure it was to have you be a part of this experience! All I had to do was ask and you were there for me in giving your opinions. To my friend Victoria Brown who had the opportunity to read my manuscript thank you so much. To my best friend, Claudette Glover, who always thought I was very talented; thank you for always being there for me. And a very special thanks to my husband, Elijah, for his patience when I would be on the computer all day and night trying to complete this book and was my big supporter. I love you all.

Table of Contents

This book is about the lives of eight women who are friends. These women stood by each other not only in good times but in bad times, as well. Their stories are being told by Kayla, who is a confidant to them all.

The Perfect Relationship

When it comes to romantic relationships and the possibility of marriage, we hope to find that special person who will stand out more than any other, that person who, when you first meet, will have your heart beating rapidly. When you are apart, you cannot wait to see them again. Just to hear their voice makes it difficult for you to contain your excitement; that perfect person who will make your life complete.

I have heard a lot of people say that there is no such thing as a perfect relationship. After being married for as long as I have, I have to disagree. There is a perfect mate for each of us, if we want there to be. They may not be right for someone else, but if the two of you work at pleasing each other, taking the imperfections along with the good, if it fits you, then you can have the perfect relationship for you. Every couple's relationship is unique to them. My opinion of perfect means the relationship is fulfilling and happy. You know that things will not always be easy and the relationship will be tested, but you stay and work it out. The ones that will survive are the ones that are built on faithfulness and trustworthiness.

My name is Kayla and I have been married for twenty years. When I look back over our relationship, I don't have any regrets. Before I was married, I set out to find the perfect man, someone who would complete me. I felt if I found the perfect man, then I could have the perfect relationship.

Is there such a thing as a perfect person, someone who can complete you?

THE PERFECT RELATIONSHIP

Let's define perfect: without faults, complete and whole, excellent, flawless, having no impurities.

THE PERFECT RELATIONSHIP

Is there anyone beside our Lord and Savior like that?

Let's stop thinking that someone can complete us and see that self-happiness is the start of finding that special someone with whom you can have true, long-lasting love. Love yourself for who you are. If you don't like who you are, then change. No one can complete you, but they may have everything that is wanted or needed to make you happy.

Some of my friends who thought they had the perfect relationship have stories to tell. I have asked them if I could share their stories in case there are other women who have gone or are going through similar relationships. They all thought that they had found their soul mate, the love of their lives, that picture-perfect mate. We all wanted to have love, to find that special someone who would be our dream man. We all believed that love is delightful and we wrote a poem for our motto:

Love Is Delightful
Love is delightful, charming and true
My life changed tremendously the day I met you.
Love is wonderful, love is kind
It enters my heart and controls my mind!
Love is enjoyable, pleasing and nice
Some like it so much they tried it twice!
You are my lover, my dream come true
Forever and ever I will love you!
You are my life, my world, my all
Always forever at your beck and call!
I thank you my love for being there

THE PERFECT RELATIONSHIP

When I needed you the most?
Your caring heart has made me whole.
Your caring ways took over my soul.
You are my perfect love!
You always speak to me in sweet honesty and truth
There is no other I could love as much as I love you!
And if our love should ever stop
I'll still not be alone. For I shall forever carry the love
You had for me imbedded deep in my soul!

And when the day is come and gone
And the night is dark and dim
The love we share shall make a light
And keep the darkness bright!
And if we ever have to part
And go our separate ways
Memories of the love we shared
Will remain in my heart always!

My friends, the women who will share their stories, are Claudia, Quiana, Camille, Carol, Kima, Marjorie, Briana and Melody.

We all are married or have been married, except Carol, who was engaged, and Briana, who is the youngest of us all. We all believe in love, but love didn't always go as we had hoped.

I am going to try and tell each of our stories as I have seen or heard it down through the years and tell you why some of us have stayed in the relationship while others have gotten divorced; walked out and left it all. I will begin with Claudia's story as she told it to me, and what I saw for myself.

CHAPTER 1

Claudia

Claudia and I have been friends for about fifteen years, we met in college. We liked each other right from the start and a friendship like no other developed. After college, Claudia and I moved to separate locations; she to Pennsylvania, I to New York. We both had relatives in those states and jobs were plentiful. She would become a social worker and I, a bank executive. A few years later, we both relocated to Virginia.

Claudia would soon meet and marry Edward, a very smart and handsome man, a college professor. This was the man of her dreams. They had been dating for two years when he asked her to marry him. She was ecstatic.

Before the wedding, everything was wonderful. Edward was so attentive, loving, kind and affectionate. Ten months after the wedding, things changed dramatically.

Claudia had been working extensively for three weeks straight. Her caseload was heavy. She was the supervisor, but she was also understaffed and had to take some additional caseloads herself. She was coming home late each night and leaving early each morning. She had explained the situation to Edward and thought he understood, but into the beginning of the third week, things started to change and she began to see a side of him that she had never seen before. Little did she know the changes that life with this man was about to take.

THE PERFECT RELATIONSHIP

Claudia had been busy all day. Usually, she would take time to call Edward just to say hello, tell him she loved him and that maybe she would be a little late coming home, if that was going to be the case. But this day was different. Every time she would pick up the phone, someone would come into her office distracting her. It was already 7 p.m. when she realized that she hadn't spoken to Edward all day. She reached for the phone to call him, but decided that she was ready to leave and would be home in thirty minutes.

Claudia was about to put her key in the lock, when the door flew open and Edward was standing there in a fury. "Where have you been? Do you know what time it is? I have left messages for you all day. Are you playing me for a fool? Who is he?" Before she could speak, he drew back and hit her so hard, she fell. Before she could move, he reached out, grabbed her by the hair and pulled her inside and continued to beat, curse and kick her. "You think I am a fool! I will teach you not to cheat on me!"

Claudia was trying to speak, but the pain was too much. "Edward, please, what are you talking about? I have been at work. I told you how busy my office is and I am understaffed." With that, he went to hit her again, but she managed to rise and ran into the bathroom and locked the door.

She couldn't believe what had just happened. This man, whom she hadn't even been married to for a year, had just beaten her. This man, whom she had prayed for, her Mr. Right, hadn't even given her a chance to explain why she was late.

She tried to compose herself. She couldn't believe that this was the man she was so madly in love with, the man she had dreamed she would marry some day.

The pain was so unbearable she could hardly move. She managed to stand and when she looked in the mirror she didn't even recognize her own face. Her right eye was blackened, her lip was busted and swollen to twice its size and her right cheek was bruised. She had to get to the hospital. Her side was hurting and she thought she might have cracked ribs.

Claudia was afraid to open the door, afraid of what Edward might do next. But she had to get out of the house; she needed medical attention.

She looked around the bathroom for something to defend herself; there was nothing. Still looking, she found an old blade that Edward used to shave with. As afraid as she was, she would surely use it if it came to that. This was and would be the last time he would ever hit her. Her father, may he rest in peace, told her, 'If a man hit you once and you stay with him, he would surely hit you again.' He also told her, 'No matter how much you think you love him, get out of the situation as fast as possible!' Claudia spoke out loud. "Daddy, that's exactly what I am going to do, right after I get medical attention."

She slowly opened the door and looked out. He was standing nearby. Whatever she did she had to be careful. She wanted to get out of the house and once out, was never coming back.

Claudia slowly walked out of the bathroom; Edward took one look at her and fell to his knees. "Oh, baby, I am sorry; I didn't mean to hurt you. I love you so much and the thought of you being with another man drives me crazy. Please forgive me; I will never hit you again."

Claudia had to be careful how she handled this. She was going to make sure he never hit her again, but first, she had to get out of there. "Edward, I have been busy for the last few weeks, I've told you that. I am married to you, I love you; we haven't even been married for a year yet, we are still newlyweds. I haven't even thought about another man since I met you. Right now, I need medical attention. I think my ribs are cracked, please take me to the hospital."

She could barely walk. Edward had to pick her up and carry her out. While in the car, Edward asked Claudia not to tell anyone that he had done this to her, that it would ruin his reputation and if the college he taught at found it out, he might get fired. "Please tell everyone you fell down the stairs," he pleaded with her. Claudia knew that as soon as she was safe in the hospital, she was going to have him arrested for assault and battery; her marriage was over.

At the hospital, as soon as Edward was asked to leave the room, Claudia told the doctor that it was her husband who had done this to her and she wanted him arrested. Edward was sitting outside the emergency room when the police officers approached him.

"Mr. Graves, are you Edward Graves? Your wife's name is Claudia?"

"Yes, officer, yes. I am Edward Graves; is there something wrong? How can I help you?"

"Please stand and put your hands behind your back; you are being arrested for assaulting your wife."

"My wife fell down the stairs, didn't she tell you that?"

"No, sir, she didn't. She said you beat her and she wanted you arrested."

The officer started to read Edward his Miranda Rights, "You have the right to remain silent. Anything you say can and will be used against you in a court of law. You have the right to speak to an attorney and to have an attorney present during any questioning. If you cannot afford a lawyer, one will be provided for you at government expense. Do you understand what you have just heard?"

"Yes," Edward answered. "Please let me see my wife, she can clear this up."

At that moment Edward saw Claudia being taken out on a stretcher, he yelled to her, "Claudia what is going on? You promised you would tell them you fell down the stairs. Do you know what you have done? If this gets out, my reputation will be ruined."

Claudia glanced over at Edward with so much sorrow, "Edward, your reputation ruined? Look at me! I have three cracked ribs, a split lip, a chipped tooth, a concussion and my right eardrum may be busted—and all you can think of is your reputation! Do you know what you have done? Our marriage is over. As soon as I am able, I am filing for divorce."

With that, Edward started to yell. "You wait, you haven't seen anything yet. Just wait until I get my hands on you; how can you do this to me? I love you, Claudia; please tell them it was an accident. Claudia, please Claudia, what will people think? I teach at a college, I can lose my job. Claudia, please, I promise, I will never hit you again. Please, Claudia!"

The officers had to tell Edward to calm down; he was yelling and threatening to harm Claudia as soon as he saw her again. "Sir, please calm down. You are only making it harder for yourself. If anything happens to your wife later, my partner here and I will have to testify to what we heard you say." With that, Edward calmed down.

Edward was taken to the precinct where he was booked. He couldn't believe he was being treated like a criminal. He felt he had done nothing wrong. So, he had hit his wife, so what? A lot of husbands hit their wives. Some of them needed it to keep them in check. But Edward knew Claudia was different. He had never met any woman like her. She was as perfect, as perfect could be and when she kept coming home late, even though she told him she was working, he was so jealous, he didn't believe her. Other men were always looking at her. He thought back to the time they were in a restaurant. She went to the lady's room, and one gentleman followed her back to the table. Even with him sitting there, the man tried to get her phone number! Edward had to tell him that she was his wife and to please leave. "What a fool I've made of myself," he thought. "I hope she will forgive me and come home. I promise I will never hit her again."

Edward didn't know whom to call to come get him out of jail. "Damn! Me, a college professor behind bars for hitting his wife. I have to keep this quiet." The only person he could call was his brother Allen. He knew that Allen would keep his mouth shut.

Allen couldn't believe what he was hearing, "You are where; you want me to come and do what?"

"Look, brother, just get here as soon as you can, and please keep this quiet. I don't want anyone to know about this."

It seemed like hours before Allen showed up at the precinct. On the way home, he had to know what had happened.

"Hey, big brother, you want to tell me what is going on; how you ended up in jail?" Edward didn't know how to start.

"Well, Claudia and I got into an argument and I hit her; well, I beat her up."

"You did what? I don't believe you hit her. And she's in the hospital! Man, I need to stop this car right now and beat the daylights out of you. I know she is your wife, but that doesn't give you the right to hit her; I don't care what she did. You know dad didn't raise us to beat on women. Edward, you have one of the sweetest wives I know and besides that, she is gorgeous and I know she loves you. What happened and how bad is it?"

"It's pretty bad. For the past few weeks, Claudia has been working late. She told me that her office is understaffed and she had to take on some of the caseloads herself. I knew she was telling the truth, but where she used to call me everyday, that day she didn't. I thought she was seeing someone."

Allen was stunned. "You two have been married less than a year. I thought you were still on your honeymoon. Look, man, I think I know Claudia a little; she would not cheat on you. Is it as bad as you say it is?"

"When I was being arrested, I saw them taking her somewhere; she looked terrible. Black eye, swollen lip and she told me she had broken ribs and maybe a broken eardrum, a concussion and a chipped tooth. I didn't want to hurt her; I just wanted her to come home. I love her so much. She is the best thing that ever happened to me, I don't want to lose her. I am going to do whatever I can to make this up to her. I just hope she will talk to me, let me explain; hear what I have to say. Do you think she will talk to me, do you think she will come back to me, come home?"

Allen spoke up, "I don't know man. I don't think Claudia is the type of woman to stay with a man who hits her. She's smart, independent and really can live without a man if she needs to, especially a man who has hurt her the way you have. I mean, come on man, chipped tooth, concussion and cracked ribs? I can't believe you did that to her. Claudia really loves you, at least she used to; after this, I don't know. Remember when you were out of town and she had car trouble? She called me to come help her. She told me how much she loved you; that she had waited what seemed forever for the right man. That she had waited on the Lord for someone special and He had sent you. Brother, I hope you haven't let jealousy ruin your marriage."

THE PERFECT RELATIONSHIP

As soon as Claudia could get to a phone, she called me. I couldn't believe what I was hearing.

"Claudia, sweetie, what do you mean you are in the hospital, that Edward beat you up? Stop crying and tell me what happened."

"Kayla, you know I love my husband and that I would never cheat on him. You know that I have been working overtime a lot lately. I've told you we are so understaffed that I am doing some of the caseloads myself. Well, Edward thinks I am with another man when I tell him I am working late. I thought I knew this man. We dated for two years before we decided to get married; he was such a gentleman. Never once did I see any anger in him, even when other men would make passes at me right in front of him. He would say they could make all the passes they wanted, that I was his woman and he knew I loved him and would never look at another man. Back then, he trusted me. What happened? The minute we said, 'I do,' he changed. Did I make a mistake by marrying this man? Kayla, you have to come to the hospital. We have been friends for so long, you are the only true friend I have. Please come, I need you."

As soon as Claudia hung up, I grabbed my purse and headed for the door. I couldn't believe what I had just heard; they seemed to be so much in love. I remembered the first time Claudia told me she had found someone so different from any man she had ever met, that he was the one that she had waited on the Lord for; that He had sent her Edward. On their wedding day, when they took their vows, they each had written something special to say to the other. It was beautiful. All the guests were crying, men and women. I guess it's true what they say about not knowing someone until you live with them.

DR. CAROLYN WHITE-BROWN

At the hospital, I was shocked to see Claudia all swollen, and she couldn't stop crying. I had to sit with her practically all night before she could calm down. "Claudia, you think maybe I should call your mother or sister? What do you want me to do?" I asked.

"Kayla, you are the only person I need right now. We have been friends forever. I know you better than I know anybody. My mother would probably find Edward and beat him to death with her walking cane. If I call my sister, Betty, she will eat this up, be happy that this happened. You know her husband hits her and she will not leave him, saying he loves her and he is always sorry for what he did. Then he takes her out and buys her furs and expensive jewelry. She tells me that it's her fault, because she didn't have dinner ready, or took to long getting ready to go out. I remember he even pushed her down the steps, because she made the mistake of walking in front of him. He told her that she is always to walk behind him. I swear, if I were married to him, I would be in jail, because I would have killed him by now. And that's why I wanted you to come here."

"Wait a minute Claudia; you aren't going to kill Edward, are you?"

"Kayla, please, I want you here because I need a place to stay. I am not going back to Edward. Our marriage is over, before it even really got started. Tell me, Kayla, how do you keep your marriage going? You and Elijah have been married forever and you two seem to be so much in love. How do you do it? Has he ever hit you or cursed at you? Please tell me how you two do it. How do you have the perfect relationship?"

"Claudia, it's quite simple. We respect each other, believe in each other, trust each other and have never missed one day telling each other that we love each other. I had a long talk with

Elijah when he asked me to marry him. Anyway, it's a long story; I'll tell you about it one day, right now let's see if we can help you. Now tell me what happened."

"I came home late last night. Edward met me at the door, saying I had been with another man; that I was cheating on him, and before I could say anything, the result is what you are looking at. I had him arrested and I hope he stays in jail. I will not live with a man who hits me. Look at me; he beat the hell out of me. If I hadn't run into the bathroom, I might not be here right now. It was terrible. While in the bathroom, I was trying to find something to fight back with and I found this old razor. I swear if he had hit me when I came out, I was going to cut him every which way but loose. I can't live like that. And you know how much I love him. I just knew God had put this man in my life, that he was the perfect man. Well, God is love and all things good; there was no love and nothing good about what Edward did to me. It's amazing; I really loved him. I am saying loved because right now, I do not love him at all. I doubt if I ever will again. Oh, Kayla, I can't go back to Edward. I remember my father telling my sister and me that if a man beats us to leave him, because if we let him get away with it one time, he would do it again. I am not going back and I mean it."

"Kayla, you should have seen Edward, he was like a mad man; I was afraid and I'm still afraid. Can I stay with you for a few days until I can get my own place? Luckily, I kept forgetting to open that joint account with Edward. I do have money of my own."

Allen had gotten Edward out of jail and they were now at Edward and Claudia's house. Edward had been in jail for almost 48 hours. What an experience; he never wanted to go there again.

Why had he hit Claudia? He knew she would never cheat on him. He had become so jealous. She was so beautiful and he wanted her all to himself. "Please, God, please let her come back home to me."

Edward was so busy thinking about Claudia that he didn't hear Allen calling him.

"Hey, bro, don't you think you should call the hospital to see how Claudia is doing? Do you want me to take you over there?"

"Let me clean up first, I don't want her to come home and be reminded of what happened."

After Edward had cleaned up, he called the hospital. He was told that Claudia had been discharged that morning.

Edward became worried, where could she be? Right away he thought, "She can only be at Kayla's" He called. Yes, Claudia is here, but she doesn't want to talk to you. Edward kept insisting that I put Claudia on the phone, but I was persistent. "Edward, please give her some time, she is in pain right now, let her rest today and tomorrow you two can talk. Please Edward, tomorrow." He agreed with me, and thought that was the best thing to do.

After Allen left, Edward continued cleaning up the house; he wanted it to be perfect when Claudia came home. He was going to make it up to her. Why did he do what he had done? He had never hit a woman before; not one, but he never loved any woman the way he loved Claudia. She was deep inside him. He found himself being jealous of her friends. He thought sometimes she loved her friends more than him, but he knew that wasn't true, that it was a different kind of love.

Claudia awoke early the next morning. She wanted to have some quiet time to herself before everyone else got up and she wanted to pray. All the bedrooms in Kayla's house have large walk in closets; she went in one, got on her knees and began to pray.

THE PERFECT RELATIONSHIP

"Our Father who art in heaven, I come to you today with a heavy heart. I need you, Father, right now to guide me. Help me do the right thing. I love my husband, but I can't and won't live with a man who will hit me. I won't live with a man who doesn't have faith enough in me to trust me. Father God, I have only been married for ten months and my husband has beaten me, he beat me, like someone would beat off a wild animal. Please, Father, tell me what to do. I thought this man was whom You had chosen for me, I never went looking for a husband. I let him find me; he sought me out. We dated for two years. He was nice, kind; he made me smile and most of all I thought he loved me, really loved me, but, Father, love doesn't hurt and he hurt me, really hurt me.

"I have given this man all of me. I felt that we were not just emotionally and physically connected, but spiritually, as well. Please, Lord, tell me what to do. I can't live with this man any more. I don't think I can ever look at him again like I used to. My goal in my marriage was to be completely committed to my husband. We were so close, we had the "oneness" relationship that You speak of in the Bible, and in one moment, he took that all away. Please, Father, I need some guidance right now. Tell me what to do. I have to face my husband today; I have to talk to him. I don't know what to do. I feel my marriage is over. I need to hear from You. In Your name, Father, I pray. Amen."

Claudia hurried and got dressed; she would wait until she knew Edward had left for his job and then she would go over to her house and pack some things, then go to the bank. She was so happy she hadn't gotten around to opening the joint account. She had her own money, twenty-five thousand dollars.

"That should be enough to help me get my own place and be okay for awhile. After what is happening to me, I believe every woman should have her own money. Thank you, Mom, for insisting that your children save for a rainy day, even if it was only two dollars a day. I have been saving since I was sixteen years old and the rainy day is here." When she thought Edward had left for work, she went to her house.

Claudia sat outside for ten minutes before she decided to go in. It was such a beautiful house; she loved it. She and Edward had looked for about six months before they found their house. They knew it was the one the minute they saw it. And when they walked inside, it was just beautiful. They were so much in love with each other. She remembered them sitting in the master bedroom on the floor holding each other and talking about their future there and the children they would have.

"Edward said he wanted them all to look like me. I said I wanted a little boy to look like him. It's good to have memories; I always thought he and I would grow old together still madly in love and sitting holding hands remembering our years together. Well, that isn't going to happen now."

Claudia got the spare key and was about to open the door when suddenly it opened. She was at first shocked and then afraid. Edward's car was in the shop, that's why it wasn't in the driveway. He had decided to take the day off. Before she could speak or move, Edward grabbed her hand and led her into the house. Claudia tried to pull back; Edward told her not to be afraid and led her into the living room and asked her to please sit. Looking at her face, he was so sorry for what he had done. Even though her face wasn't as swollen as it had been, it was still scarred; her eye was still black and her lip was still a little swollen. He tried to put his arms around her, but she jumped from the pain in her ribs.

Edward fell to his knees crying. "Oh, Claudia, baby, I am so sorry; please tell me you will forgive me. I love you so much, I promise I will never hit you again; please tell me you are here to stay. Please, Claudia, I can't live without you. I will make this up to you. Please talk to me, baby, please. What do you want me to do, do you still love me?"

Claudia was afraid to answer. If she said the wrong thing, Edward might get upset and hit her again. "Right now, I need some time to myself; I am going to stay at Kayla's for awhile, maybe a week or two. I have to think about this, really think about this."

"But, Claudia," exclaimed Edward, "what is there to talk about? I've told you I am sorry, that I love you and I promised I will never hit you again!" Reaching for her hand, he said, "Baby, I love you so much, this is our home, please don't leave, if you go, I feel you are never coming back."

Little did he know that was exactly what was going to happen. Once she got her things out of the house, she was never coming back, but she wasn't going to tell Edward that right now. She had to be smart and let him think she was coming home. She felt if she told him she wasn't, he would get angry and next time she wouldn't be so lucky.

She took another approach. "Edward, I just need a little time to myself, that's all. Please give me that, I need time to heal. You sit here and tell me you love me, but I want to think about that, because love doesn't cause a husband to beat up his wife. Love doesn't cause a husband to call his wife a bitch; love doesn't hurt. Look at me, is this how you show your love? All you had to do was trust me, have enough faith in me to know that I would never cheat on you. You say you love me, but I think you love me not. Please let me have a little time to think about what happened. I will be at Kayla's. But promise me you will not call me; give me time to think this over. I promise I will call you and then we can talk."

Edward was scared, he knew Claudia was sincere in what she was saying now, but he knew her well. She wasn't telling him everything. Why didn't he trust her when she told him she was working, but most of all why did he hit her? If there was a perfect marriage, he thought it was theirs. Now he had ruined it. He could feel it in his heart; deep down he knew their relationship would never be the same.

His thoughts went back to the very first moment he saw her. He loved every little thing about her. Her cute smile, magical eyes, the way she walked and the sound of her voice. Her gentle touch and the warmth he felt when he was with her. He was going to do everything possible to get back what they had.

Claudia was thankful that all had gone well with her and Edward, but she knew that it would never be the same—and from the look in Edward's eyes, he knew it, too. "Oh, God, why did this have to happen, why couldn't he trust me?"

She also remembered the day they first met. He was the most incredible man she had ever met. She had waited it seemed forever to meet someone like him. He, she thought, was perfect. He was a gentleman, loving, caring and never pressuring her to do anything she didn't want to do. He told her that he knew she was born to be his wife; that God had made her just for him, and later when he asked her to marry him, he promised to always take care of her, never doubt her and protect her. Now, she thought, she had to call the police to protect her from him; and as for never doubting her, well, she had a sore body to show otherwise.

At the bank, Claudia closed the account she had and went to another bank to open an account there. She didn't want to run into Edward at their current bank later. She was so sad; husband and wife are supposed to share. They had planned on opening a joint account with the money she had saved when she was single and they would have that in case of an emergency or a start to help with their children's education. She wanted children very much. Now, with Edward, she didn't know. She had to make one more stop; it was to see her pastor, Reverend Williams.

She and Edward had gone to counseling before they were married. Pastor Williams had given them some excellent advice then. She needed some advice now; she wanted to talk to him.

Pastor Williams was in his study when she arrived at the church; he was happy to see her.

"Claudia, what happened to you? Your face; were you in an accident?"

Claudia got right to the point. "Pastor Williams, I hope you aren't too busy to speak to me, there is something of great importance I have to speak to you about."

"Come right in, my child, take a seat. How are you? Is there something wrong with Edward? You usually come in together."

"Pastor, I don't know where to start, so I will start by saying that no, I was not in an accident. Edward did this to me." She told him the whole story.

Pastor Williams had to get up and go over to Claudia as she was crying uncontrollably. "Pastor, I don't understand, I thought he loved me and trusted me. I was working late and told him that. He thought I was with another man. I was telling him the truth; I would never cheat on my husband. I thought our marriage was solid. He didn't even give me time to open the door, he just started to hit me and call me the B word. I need your advice, Pastor. Right now, I am staying with a friend. I've told Edward that I need time to think things out. The truth, Pastor, is that I will not live with a man who is abusive and has called me out of my name. Pastor Williams, please tell me what to do. I love my husband, but when he beat me the way he did, I lost some of that love. I just want to get as far away from him as I can. We have only been man and wife for ten months. My heart has changed. How any woman can stay with a man who has beat her I can't understand. But I have to go. I can't live with my husband anymore."

"Claudia, I am your pastor. Yes, I counseled you and Edward before you were married. I wanted you to know what marriage is. I wanted you to know that marriage is a gift from God, a cooperative effort between equal mates, a challenge to each of you. I wanted you to know that trials and tribulations come with marriages, as do with most anything else. Right now, you have a major problem, your husband has hit you and you want to leave him. You have come here for me to advise you what to do. I will advise you, but I will not advise you to leave him, or stay with him. I want you to listen to what I have to say and then you and your husband must talk and then you will decide what you will do.

"First, I want you to make sure that Jesus is in the midst of it and he will lead you to make the right decision. Use Jesus as an example of how to handle your feelings, remember He cares. In the book of John, it tells us about many of Jesus' emotions. He often expressed deep emotion and we must never be afraid to reveal our true feelings to Him. He will understand them, for He experienced them. You must be honest and don't leave anything out when you talk to Him. He cares for you. You must meditate; find a quiet, solitary place to pray. And fast. Your strength will come from the Lord, but you must go to Him."

"Pastor Williams, thank you. I needed to hear what you have told me. I will see you in church on Sunday; thank you again and God bless."

Claudia went back to Kayla's house. What a friend she had in Kayla. She knew Kayla was a true friend and would always be there for her, but tomorrow she would find an apartment for herself. Right now, she was going to take Pastor William's advice. She went into the living room to get the Bible she knew Kayla always kept open on the coffee table. She turned to Ephesians 5:32-33 which says that a man must love his wife as he loves himself and the wife must respect her husband; that the union of husband and wife should merge them in such a way that nothing can affect one without affecting the other. They become one, but it does not mean losing your personality in the personality of the other; but caring for your spouse as you would for yourself.

Claudia began to cry after reading that. "How could Edward love me? He says he loves me, but after what he has done, I know he doesn't."

Her thoughts went once again back to when they first met. It was a Sunday afternoon, at a fellowship program. It was "bring a friend" day and a member of the church had asked Edward to come. He was so spiritual; she liked him right away. They couldn't stop staring at each other. Finally, he came over to her and said hello. She knew right then that he was the one, her soul mate.

From that day forward they were inseparable; they became friends, did almost everything together and would talk on the phone for two or three hours a day. She remembered one time they talked for five hours straight. When she told this to her friends, no one believed her but Kayla. She said that Elijah was away on a business trip once and they had talked from 9 p.m. to 3 a.m. the next morning. Wow! She had always wanted a relationship like Kayla had...and Claudia thought she did.

After praying and mediating, Claudia called Edward and told him that they should meet to talk. He wanted her to come home, but she told him that she would rather meet at "Marie's restaurant, the one they called theirs, so that they could talk and have dinner. Edward agreed and told her he would meet her at 7 p.m.

Claudia took special care in selecting what she would wear when meeting Edward. She wanted him to really look at her, to see the person she was, to see how much love she had for him and to see the woman that he was going to lose.

Before getting out of the car, Claudia took one more look at herself in the car's visor mirror. Satisfied, she went into the restaurant. She saw Edward from across the room. She didn't want to toy with him, but she wanted him to really have a good look at her. She knew he liked the way she walked, so she made sure he saw every move. She was wearing a dress that he had picked out and it showed every curve of her body. The dress was neither too tight nor too short. She wore her hair the way he liked it, in a ponytail. She saw him looking at her; she almost felt sorry for him. She wanted him to get a good look so she slowed down her walk a little.

Edward saw Claudia the minute she drove into the parking lot, he watched her as she looked into the visor mirror and when he saw she was wearing a dress he had picked out, he knew that this was going to be a beautiful evening. As she walked towards him, it made his heart beat faster, she was a beautiful woman and his wife and he would do everything possible to win her back.

Claudia was now standing at Edward's table. He rose and went to embrace her, but she pulled back and took her seat.

"You look beautiful tonight, but you always look beautiful. You are the prettiest woman I know, and Claudia, I am so happy that you are my wife. I can't stop thinking about you when we are apart. I need you by my side. You complete me. You mean the world to me. You are the best thing that has ever happened to me. When I look at you and see what I did, it hurts me so much. Please, please, tell me that you will forgive me. Let's order and we will talk and then we can go over to Kayla's and get your things."

Edward called the waiter over and began to order what he knew to be Claudia's favorite dish. But as he started to tell the waiter what he thought Claudia would want, she stopped him and told him she would order herself and asked the waiter to bring her something different than what Edward was going to order. This took Edward by surprise but he didn't comment on it and ordered his meal. He didn't want to do anything to upset her.

When the food arrived, Edward began to talk. "Claudia, I am so happy that you came tonight. I was afraid you weren't going to come. Just having you here has made me very happy. I am so sorry for hurting you. I had promised to love honor, cherish and protect you and I didn't do that. Please forgive me. The thought of losing you is tearing me apart. Please say you forgive me and come back home. The house is so empty without you. It's not a home anymore, just a house. There is no warmth there. Please, Claudia, I love you so much. It was love that made me hit you. The thought of you being with someone else drives me crazy, but if you come back, I know I can control it. I know now that you would never cheat on me, but, baby, I love you so much, you are so deep inside of me that it makes me think stupid things. Please come home, I need to feel you beside me, to hold you in my arms. I love the way you would curl up to me and lay your head on my chest; I miss that. I love when you wake up in the morning with your hair all over your face. I would watch you get dressed; the way you combed your hair, just a bit of lipstick and you were perfect. The way you smelled and the way you would kiss me when you left, I would rush to the door to see you walk to your car. I am losing my mind living without you. Please come home."

"Edward," Claudia interrupted. "Please stop, look at my face and tell me that you hit me because you love me. Come and put your arms around me, feel the bandages that are wrapped around my ribs and look at my tooth, which now has a cap. You love me? You love me? As a little girl, I would dream of what my husband would be like. When I first met you, I thought I had found the man of my dreams and when you told me you loved me and asked me to marry you, it was a dream come true. I thought that I would never find a love that was as strong as ours. I knew that you were the person I wanted to spend the rest of my life with, the person I wanted to marry, the person I wanted to have babies with and the person I wanted to grow old with. Since day one, we've shared something incredible, something that most people only dream of. You made me the happiest I had ever been. You were a sincere, caring, loving man and I wouldn't have traded you for the world. I was so thankful and blessed that you loved me as much as I loved you and that you made me your wife, but you didn't trust me.

"We have been married less than a year. Tell me what happened and tell me why you lost your trust in me. Tell me why you didn't believe what I was telling you. Edward, a woman—whether single or married—will never cheat on her man if she knows she is the center of his world. I knew that, Edward. I knew I was the center of your world. But right now, I am not feeling you at all and right now I don't want to be your wife. You see right now, Edward, I don't trust you. You sit here and tell me that you hit me because you love me; well, you need to come over here and let me beat the living daylights out of you, because I love you, too. Yes, I love you; I can't shut my love for you off because of what has happened, but I can't live with you either. I won't live with a man who loses control and goes into a jealous rage when he feels something is going on. I like my job and there are going to be a lot of nights that I may be late coming home. I need my husband to trust me, to understand that I have a career and there may be times when I have to work late, but have the faith and confidence in me to know that my career will always be second to him."

Claudia was now crying. "Edward, I am sorry, but I can't come back to you. I have loved you like I have never loved anyone in my life before. When we met, it was like we both had hit the lottery—neither one of us was perfect, but we were perfect for each other. You are intelligent, funny and you made me happy. But after what has happened, I don't know if I can ever love you like I did and I can't live with you right now; maybe never."

Edward also was crying. He couldn't help it. Here was the woman, his wife whom he loved so dearly and she was not coming home. "Claudia, I promise, please don't say that you may not ever come back to me. If it's time you want, I will let you have your space right now but please, baby, don't leave me. I love you and I can't live without you. I love you so much that the fear of losing you makes me so sad that my heart feels like it's about to burst out of my chest. I am begging you; please don't give up on me, if I could take that night back I would. I would have done it all differently. I would have never put my hands on you."

DR. CAROLYN WHITE-BROWN

"Well, Edward, you did and I need time to heal from this ordeal you have put me through; time to think about my future. I need time to think about whether I want to save this marriage. I look back on the night this happened; you were so angry. Have you thought about what you did, what you said? You took your fist and hit me harder than I have ever been hit in my life, knocked me down, kicked me and called me a bitch. And then had the nerve to ask me—in all the pain I was in—to say I fell down the stairs. You treated me like I was an animal, a dog, not your wife. And that's what hurts so badly. I did nothing wrong. All you could think about was your reputation. I heard you yelling when the police were arresting you, saying that I would be sorry if I didn't do what you asked. I heard one of the officers telling you to calm down, that if anything happened to me, they would come looking for you because of what you were saying and you sit there telling me you love me and it won't happen again? Look at me Edward! Do I look like a fool to you?"

"No, baby, you are certainly not a fool and once again I am asking for your forgiveness. I was wrong. I want us to get back to where we were. I love you being my wife; I like saying 'my wife.' I love everything about you—your smile, the way you talk, your laugh, your eyes, hair, mouth, nose, even when you get angry at me, I love it. Our love was so grand, our love making, spectacular. Do you want to lose that? Take all the time you want, we can go to counseling. Pastor Williams helped us before we were married, maybe he can help us now. Just don't give up on us."

Claudia had to take a good look at her husband; he seemed so lost at that moment, like a little boy. She had to pinch her thigh to come back. "Okay, girl," she thought, "Don't let that puppy dog face get to you. Remember, he is the reason things are like they are right now. Our love before this had been one to cherish, we had whispered our truths to each other. My husband before this was fun, funny and intelligent; and he wanted nothing but happiness for me, for us. He didn't compete with me and he was so self-assured that he gave me space to be who I am, independent, strong and opinionated. What happened to him? The first time I don't call him he goes over the edge. Would he do it again?" She had to think about that.

She remembered what Pastor Williams had told her about marriage, that it is a gift from God, that it is a challenge for both partners and they should look for ways to restore the marriage rather than destroy it. With this in mind, she knew what she must say.

"Edward, I want you to listen to what I am about to tell you. First, I am no longer staying with Kayla. I have gotten an apartment."

Before she could go on, Edward spoke up, "Why?"

"Please let me finish. I need to be by myself right now. There is so much pain. I never expected this. I mean, not even a year of being married and we are separated. I can't live with you right now. I feel like I don't even know you; and the truth is, I am afraid that you might hit me again.

"I have a very demanding job that I like very much, but have never put it before you. I needed you to be there for me, to trust me, have faith and know that I loved you enough to never cheat on you, to be understanding about my job like I am with yours and remember that you have absolutely no reason to be jealous.

"I have to do this and I am asking that you take some time and think about what you have done. You caused this, not me. I am not saying this to hurt you, or to upset you, but our separation is your fault. And if we never get back to where we were, it is your fault, but I will try, you have my word, I will try. But I should tell you it won't be easy for me. I want you to not call me. I will call you when I am settled in and give you my address. I am not going to hide from you, I am just asking for some space right now and I need you to give me that."

Edward wasn't too happy with what Claudia had just presented to him. He wanted her home, but he knew she was right and understood what she was saying. He knew now that he could trust her. He knew it before, too, but was so jealous he wasn't thinking straight. God, he loved her and he was going to do whatever it took to get her back.

"Okay, Claudia, I will give you my word. I will let you have your space and it will give me time to think about what I have done. I want you to know that I spoke with Pastor Williams today and I am going to start counseling next week. I love you and I want you home, in our home, the house that we picked out together. I don't like the idea of you having an apartment. Is it in a safe neighborhood? Is there parking? I don't want you walking by yourself at night, parking far from the apartment."

"It's fine, it's downtown, has a doorman and parking. I can walk to my office from there. It's a one bedroom. Two of my staff members live there; that is how I found it. I will be getting my phone in a few days; I will call you and give you the number."

"Okay, Claudia, I just want you to be safe. Does your staff know what happened?"

"Yes, Edward, I did not lie to them. They see the scars and the way I am walking. Look, I am not going to sugarcoat this. Right now, I only care about my feelings and how I am handling this. Right now, I am putting myself first.

"My mother knows what happened and I can tell you right now, she is furious with you. I haven't spoken to my sister, Betty, but I am sure Mom has told her. I wasn't going to tell either of them, I only called Kayla. I knew Mom would be furious, she and Daddy always told Betty and me that if a man hit us to leave and never look back. And both of us are being hit by our husbands! Thank God that Daddy is not here to see it."

Edward was listening to Claudia, but thinking about her mother. He really liked his mother–in-law. They got along well and he didn't want her to think the worst of him. Now, her sister, Betty, was a different story. Her husband, Raymond, was always hitting her. He didn't want to be compared to Raymond; he was not like that at all.

Claudia was ready to go, it was getting late and she had told Edward that she wanted to go by the house to get some clothes; she was a little afraid to be in the house with Edward, but she was going to trust him.

Edward was true to his word; he let her get what she needed, walked her to her car, asked if she had her cell phone and asked her to call him when she was at the apartment. He almost said home, but their house was her home. He waited by the phone to hear from her. True to her word, she called him to let him know she was in the apartment.

He felt so alone. What had he done; had he messed up the best thing that had ever happened to him? Could he save his marriage? He sure wanted to and was going to do whatever it took to get his wife back. Before going to bed, he got down on his knees and began to pray.

"Heavenly Father, I know You are surprised to hear from me. I haven't prayed in a long time and I apologize for not doing so. I come to You tonight asking for forgiveness, to make

30 | P a g e

restitution to correct the problem I have caused by my actions. Lord, I love my wife. I waited and prayed for her. I do believe that You created her just for me; that it was You who guided us to each other. I am so sorry for hurting her; I would do anything to take it back. Please, Lord, help me to not be so jealous of her. You have given me the power of love and I am destroying it. I don't know what is happening to me. I just love her so much. I thank You, Father, for bringing her into my life and for allowing me to experience such a beautiful love. Grant me the kind of love that will draw happiness into my life once again. I pray that my wife will forgive me and let me back into her life. I can't change the past, but I can surely change my ways. Please, Father, hear my prayers. In your name, Father. Amen."

The next day, Edward felt a little better, but he missed Claudia terribly. He wanted so much to call her, but he had promise to give her time and space. He was so afraid she would never come back to him.

He kept going back to that night, if only he had remained calm. He should have known that Claudia would do nothing to hurt their marriage. She wasn't the type of woman to fool around, he knew that, but she was so beautiful inside and out. She was a virgin when they got married. If she didn't fool around before she was married, why would she do it after getting married? He knew she had dated before and she had told him that she had once come close to getting engaged, but decided against it because the man seemed to be a little too jealous, that if she married him he might become abusive. So, she stopped seeing him. And she ended up with a husband who was abusive to her anyway.

A week had gone by before he heard from Claudia again. She called to give him her house phone number and address. He asked if maybe they could have dinner again, she said maybe soon.

THE PERFECT RELATIONSHIP

She said she had to go and hung up before he could say anything
else. He felt so alone, he knew it was his fault and at that moment,
he decided he was going to do whatever possible to win Claudia
back. He had her address, he was going to write her a letter, and in
fact, he was going to write a letter everyday if that was what it
took. She said she wanted space; she didn't say he couldn't write.
After another few days had gone by and he hadn't heard from her,
he wrote his first letter; not too long, just enough to tell her he
loved her. He was going to fight for his marriage.

"My Darling Wife,

*A day without you in my life is like a day without sunshine,
a day without food, a day without air. I need you; my life is
empty without you. Please tell me you won't give up on us.
I need you in my life.*

*With all my love,
Edward"*

After a few days, he didn't hear from her, so he kept
writing:

"Dearest Claudia,

*I want you to know that I've fallen deeply in love
with you all over again. There are no words to express the
gratitude I feel in my heart that you came into my life and
made every day so special. You are my wife, my life, my
heart, my soul. You are my best friend, my one true love,
my one and only. I love you more today than I did*

yesterday and I'll love you more tomorrow than I do today. Loving you is the only thing that makes life worth living. Day by day, my love for you becomes overwhelming and I can't handle it when I don't see or talk to you. Please say you love me.

Love you always,
Edward"

Still, he didn't hear from her. He continued to write.

"Dearest Claudia,

I know that I have hurt you and I am so sorry for what I've done. I am asking for your forgiveness and hoping that you will come back to me and we can start all over again. I have been thinking a lot lately about what happened and it makes me feel terrible. I really cherish those moments when everything was going great. We were so happy. I ruined our happy home. We can work this out and once again bring happiness back into our lives, our home. I am determined to keep you in my life. I am nothing without you. You are the most important person in my life. Please, baby, come back to me.

Love always,
Edward"

It had now been three months since he had last spoken to Claudia. She wasn't even coming to church. He would rush there every Sunday and again for prayer service on Wednesday night.

Where was she? He had seen her mother and sister; neither would tell him where she was. The first time he had seen his mother-in-law after what had happened, he was so afraid she was going to tell him off. Instead she asked if after church they could go and talk. He was a little surprised—he knew how she felt about a man hitting a woman, especially one of her daughters. They went to a little coffee shop down the street from the church.

Once they were seated, she spoke. "Edward, what happened? Of all the young married couples I know, you and Claudia, I thought, would never be the ones going through what you are going through. When Claudia told me, you had beaten her like someone beats a dog, I was furious, and when I saw her, I became enraged. Tell me what happened. I thought you loved her."

"Mom, first, I am so sorry for what I did. And yes, I do love Claudia. I love her with all my heart. I want her to come home so badly. And I want you to know that I will never hit her again. I am so ashamed of what I did, and because of it, I may have lost the only woman that makes my life worth living.

"Mom, you know how Claudia feels about her job. Well, she told me that she was understaffed, had to take on some of the caseloads herself and would be home late. She would call me everyday. That day she didn't. I was jealous; I hadn't heard from her, I thought she was with another man. I was waiting for her.

"When I heard her car in the driveway, I opened the door. Before she knew what was going on I was all over her. It was bad. I wouldn't blame her if she never came back. But I want her, I love her and I am doing whatever I can to win her back. I love her so much. Do you know where she is?"

"Yes, son, I know where she is, but I am not going to tell you. When and if she is ready, I am sure she will call you. I wanted to hear from you what happened, and I don't have to tell you that I don't like it. I stay out of my children's business, but God knows sometimes I want to interfere. When I saw my daughter's face and the pain she was in, I wanted to come over to your house and beat the hell out of you with my cane. Thank God, I am a Christian woman.

"My husband never put his hands on me, never, and always told his daughters to leave and never come back if they married a man that did. I know he is turning over in his grave to know that both of his daughters are being abused by their husbands. Whatever happens in the future is between you, Claudia and the Lord above. I'll see you Wednesday night. Goodbye, Son."

"Mom, wait, you have spoken with Claudia; do you think she will come back to me?"

"Son, I can't answer that. I do know that she is angry, very angry. She trusted you to protect her, but instead she had to call the police to protect herself from you; but I know also that she loves you. You are just going to have to wait and see. Son, why don't you put everything in the hands of our Lord and Savior? Now I have to go."

"Where was Claudia, she said she would call, why hasn't she?" No sooner than he said that, his cell phone rang. He looked at the caller ID. It was Claudia. He was in such a rush to answer it; he dropped the phone. When he picked it up, the connection was lost? The phone rang again and he answered it. "Hello?"

"Hello, Edward, it's me Claudia, I need to see you. Can we have dinner tonight?" Edward was overjoyed. "Yes. Marie's—or is there some place else?"

"No, Marie's is fine."

"Okay, I'll see you at seven."

35 | P a g e

Edward was the happiest he had been in a while. He hadn't heard from Claudia in three months. He had promised to give Claudia space and time and he didn't want to do anything to have her angry with him and not come back ever. He was going to do whatever she wanted to get her back.

He was like a woman picking out his clothes. He couldn't decide what he should wear. He wanted to look nice for her. He decided to wear some clothes they had picked out together. Brown slacks with a brown tweed sports jacket to match and he put on cologne he knew she liked.

Edward was hoping that Claudia was ready to come back home. He had done everything he could to win her back; he had written love letters, gone to counseling with Pastor Williams and was now in therapy. He had gone to the president of the college he taught at and told him what happened. Better he tells him than for him to hear it from someone else. He had really messed up and he was the only one who could fix it. Before Edward left for the restaurant, he prayed.

"Heavenly Father, I come to you praying that tonight my wife and I will reconcile and restore our marriage. Please let her see that I love her and will never hurt her again. Please let her see the change in me and how sorry I am for what I did. I truly miss her and want her home. Please let her see how regretful I am for what I did to her. And give me strength to understand if she never wants to come back to me. In your name, Father. Amen."

Edward was so nervous. Claudia was already there. He parked next to her car. She was early, maybe that was a good sign and maybe she was ready to come home.

Claudia was waiting for Edward at their favorite table. Was that a coincidence or had she asked for it? He was so nervous; it was like he was meeting her for the first time. He walked up to the table, bent down and kissed her on the cheek; she didn't pull away. Now that was a good sign.

"Hi Claudia, I hope you weren't waiting long. You did say seven, o'clock didn't you?"

"Hi Edward, no, I just got here. You look nice, smell nice, too. I miss your smell."

Edward thought, "She is missing me." He asked, "Do you want something to drink?" He motioned for the waiter. "The lady will have a glass of Chardonnay and I will have Chablis please. Is that alright, Claudia? I know you like your wine white and dry."

"Edward, it's fine. You know I always liked you ordering for me. I love it when you say, 'the lady.' It makes me feel so respected. Why don't you order my dinner for me? Let's see if you still remember."

"We have only been separated for three months. I could never forget anything about you, and you look beautiful tonight."

"Thank you, Edward. You look very handsome and you are wearing my favorite pants and jacket.

"Edward, I asked you here tonight because I feel it's time we talked. First, I want you to know that I took some time off and went on a little vacation. No, there wasn't any man. I went with my girlfriends. You know them all, Kayla, Quiana, Camille, Carol, Kima, Marjorie, Briana and Melody. They all thought I needed to get away for awhile, so they all packed up and went with me to Paris."

"Paris, France? That's where we went on our honeymoon."

"Yes, I had to go back there. That was one of the best times in my life. Being in Paris with the man I love, my husband. I was trying to see if I could feel what I felt when I was with you. And the answer is no. Edward, I had my friends with me. But they weren't you. I was miserable; in fact, I have been miserable for the past three months.

"I have been seeing Pastor Williams for counseling, he told me that he is seeing you also; well, I feel that we should go together now. I needed my time alone first and I am sure you did, also. There were some things I had to figure out and if you had been there I don't think I would have been able to. Are you willing to be counseled together now?"

"Claudia, I want us back together so badly, I will do anything." He reached and took her hand. "I love you so much." He had tears in his eyes. "Please come home; I will never doubt your word again and I will never hurt you again."

"Edward, I love you, too, I never stopped. I just had some things to sort out. I don't want to keep saying this to you and after tonight I promise I won't, but you hurt me, not just physically, but emotionally and mentally. What you did to me was tearing me apart. I was losing it. I hated you and I was never going to forgive you. Thank God for my mother, my friends and Pastor Williams. I was blaming myself for what happened. But Edward I am not to blame, you are.

"I want you to listen to what I am going to say and if you agree, we can get through this. First, I forgive you. Now this doesn't mean that I am denying your responsibility for hurting me and it doesn't lessen or excuse the wrong I am forgiving you for—I am not excusing the act. I had so much hate in me for what you had done, that I was making myself sick. I was unhappy, wasn't able to do my job and wasn't eating. I had to reclaim my freedom and the only way to do that was to release my anger and forgive you. And it wasn't easy, but with the help of God, I am not bitter anymore, the resentment is gone."

Edward couldn't believe what he was hearing; he didn't know what to say. "Oh, baby, I am so happy. I thought I had lost you."

"Edward, it was God's grace that saved me and helped me to forgive you. Last night I was taking off my rings, I had so much resentment that I was going to throw my wedding rings in the trash. As I was about to drop them in the garbage, God spoke to me and gave me two scriptures to read. The first one was Song of Solomon 8:6, it tells of the power of love. It says that "love is as strong as death." Love cannot be killed by time or disaster and it cannot be bought for any price, because it is freely given. Love is priceless, and even the richest king cannot buy it. Love must be accepted as a gift from God and then shared within the guidelines that God provides.

"The second scripture comes from Ecclesiastes 4:9-12. It states that life is designed for companionship, not isolation. For intimacy, and not loneliness. We are not here on earth to serve ourselves; however, but to serve God and others. Don't isolate yourself and try to go it alone. Seek companions; be a team member. I then thought of our wedding vows: for better or worse, in sickness and in health, for richer or for poorer, till death do us part.

"I do not want to be alone any longer. I want to come back home. As a matter of fact, I have all my things in the car. But once back there you have to be patient with me. I am coming home, but it's going to take time for me to really come back to you. I know I love you, but I can't rush back into your arms. I feel that if we are going to work this out, then we can work it out together in our home, where our love was good and strong. And, Edward, you must trust me when I am not with you, when I am late coming home. And you may not like what I am going to say next, but you have to promise me that you will get anger management counseling. I won't go through this again. What are your thoughts?"

Edward was so happy that he wanted to rush over to Claudia and hold her in his arms, but he knew for now that he had to keep his distance. All he could say was, thank you, thank You. I'll do whatever it takes to save our marriage."

After dinner, they went out to their cars and he followed her home." Home" he thought; finally, their house was going to be a home again.

Once they were at home and it was time for bed, Edward took Claudia's things in the guest bedroom. Claudia saw him and asked him to please put then in the master bedroom, that there was where she would be sleeping, that she had missed her bed.

As they got into bed, she asks him to be patient with her, if they could just lay in each other's arms like they used to; sort of get used to each other all over again. And, eventually, the lovemaking would come. He was happy just to have her home. He knew it would take time before she let him have her again, but he was patient. Just holding her, smelling her, was wonderful.

Just before Claudia fell asleep, she put her head on Edward's chest and recited a verse from her favorite poem:

"And when the day is come and gone,
And the night is dark and dim
The love we share shall make a light
And keep the darkness bright!"

Claudia and Edward have been married now for ten years and seem to be so much in love; it seems that what they went through made their marriage stronger. It's amazing what some of us go through in our relationships. All Edward had to do was trust Claudia and believe in her to believe in them.

Relationships are all about trust. Trust to know that your partner has your back. Trust to know that you can rely on them to do the right thing, that they will be devoted to you and respect the relationship. If the bonds are deep, far down within your soul, then the relationship will be strong and nothing will be able to break the bond. But if you don't have that bond, that trust, the relationship is weak and won't last.

Being able to trust each other is very important in a relationship. Most of us, I am sure, have had negative thoughts about what the other is doing when apart. If the relationship is going to last, trust must be in it. You must have confidence in yourself first and then confidence in your mate to know that they will not do anything to harm the union. Trust is the foundation for a relationship to build on.

If your relationship is going to work, you need to be able to trust each other with your past, your present and your hopes and dreams for the future. Trust takes time and effort, is easily broken and is hard to restore, but if you're willing to work at it, the reward is the relationship you've always hoped for and what you will have is imperfect people creating a perfect relationship.

Chapter 2

Quiana

After 15 years of marriage, Quiana felt she no longer loved her husband and wanted to end the marriage. When she looked back over their marriage, she had to sit down and pray to God to give her strength to do what she had to do. Surely it was not going to be easy. "Please, God," she prayed. "I am so sorry, but I have to tell Stanley. I have to let him know I want out of this marriage. What happened to the love we had 15 years ago?" She had adored Stanley and he, her. Her thoughts went back to when they first met.

She had been shopping all day trying to find the right dress to wear to her cousin's wedding. The wedding was going to take place in three days and she was rushing to get the perfect dress. She usually was not a last-minute person, but being a play writer/director, her work schedule for the past three months had kept her very busy with rehearsals for a new play to be performed for the first time.

Her hands were full of packages when she reached her car. She had forgotten to take her keys out while inside the store, now she was standing at her car fumbling around in her purse for them. Out of the corner of her eye, she saw a man coming towards her. She panicked and dropped her purse and packages. She was about to scream, but decided to pray instead. The man was getting closer. Quiana prayed, "The Lord is my light and my salvation; whom shall I fear? The Lord is the strength of my life; of whom shall I be afraid? When the wicked, even mine enemies and my foes, came upon me to eat my flesh, they stumbled and fell."

The man, hearing Quiana praying, yelled out to her. "Are you Quiana Roberts?" Hearing her name, Quiana responded, "Why yes, I am Quiana Roberts. And who may I ask are you, have we met before?"

"My name is Stanley, Stanley Whitehead. I was walking behind you in the store. When you opened the door to come out you dropped your credit card. I picked it up and called out to you, but you were walking so fast, you didn't hear me. That is how I knew your name. I am sorry I scared you."

"You didn't scare me," Quiana told him. "The Lord is my light and my salvation, whom shall I fear?" With that, they both laughed.

"Let me help you with your packages, and here is your card." They picked up the packages and he turned to walk away, when Quiana called out to him.

"Mr. Whitehead, thanks. And yes, you did scare me." He smiled the most beautiful smile she had ever seen. They both said goodbye, got into their cars and drove off.

At home later that evening, Quiana couldn't stop thinking about Stanley Whitehead—and what a name! She spoke out loud, "Quiana Roberts-Whitehead."

"Oh, girl," she thought, "you will probably never see that man again, but what a handsome man he is." She also had noticed that he was a little older, how much older she didn't know. "Oh well, he is probably married. Anyway, he was just a stranger who was nice enough to return my credit card."

Three days after the incident in the mall parking lot, no matter how she tried, Quiana couldn't get Stanley Whitehead out of her head. She wished there was some way she could find him, but how would that happen? He probably hadn't given her a second thought.

"Today," she spoke out loud, "is my cousin Micaiah's wedding and I have to focus on that and forget about Mr. Stanley Whitehead. I must get dressed now; I don't want to be late for the wedding of the year."

Quiana was one of the first guests to arrive at the church, and she was beautiful. She wore a red dress. Even though it was store-bought, it fit as if it had been made especially for her. When she had walked out of her house to her car, her neighbor's 15-year-old son, Keyron, and all his friends, came over to say hello to her. They all stared and asked her if they could help her into her car. She had to laugh to herself. When she drove off, Keyron told his friends, "I sure wish I was old enough to ask Miss Roberts out, she is so pretty."

Her mother was always asking her why she didn't have a boyfriend and if she was ever going to get married. Quiana hated when her mother would say to her, "Girl, you are a beautiful Black woman. What is wrong with you? As pretty as you are, you are going to end up an old maid."

She was all into her thoughts when cousin Micaiah came up to her. "Hey, little cousin, you look beautiful. That's some dress you are wearing. Be careful now, we don't want you looking as good as my bride. I must say that beside my bride, you will be the prettiest woman here. Oh, by the way, there is someone I want you to meet. He should be here any minute; he left something in the car. I want you to know that he is a little older than you, but I think you two will make a great couple. Where were you last Sunday? I wanted to introduce him to you then, but you were not in church.

He is the new assistant pastor and he is marrying me today. We went to college together."

"Thanks cousin, but no thanks. A preacher man? For me? Please, I don't think so." Quiana turned to walk away and looked right into Stanley Whitehead's face. Before she could say anything, Micaiah was speaking. "Man, what took you so long? Come meet my beautiful cousin. Quiana, this is the preacher man I was telling you about."

"Well, hello, Quiana. Nice to see you again."

"Hi Stanley, nice to see you also."

"Wait a minute," said Micaiah, "you two know each other?"

"This is the pretty lady I was telling you I met in the mall parking lot." He looked directly into Quiana's eyes, "And speaking of pretty, you look beautiful today."

"I can't believe this," said Micaiah. "Here I am trying to put you two together and you have already met."

"It was just for a few minutes," said Stanley, "and you never asked me her name. But right now, before I marry you and Calyiah, I am going to get this lady's phone number—if she will give it to me and if she doesn't mind me calling her later."

"Look you two," Micaiah cut in, "you have only a few minutes to acquaint yourselves again. Remember, today is my day."

The wedding was beautiful. Calyiah was the most gorgeous bride. She and Micaiah made a good-looking couple.

Quiana was happier than she had been in a long time. Stanley stayed by her side during the entire reception. She had finally met someone she liked very much, an older man and a preacher. Could this be her Mr. Right? She couldn't wait to tell her mother; she saw how she kept staring at them at the reception and trying to get her to tell her what was going on. She thought she would let her mother suffer a little while longer. She would call her tomorrow and tell her all about it. She was tired now and just wanted to take a hot bubble bath and think about this man she was about to let into her life.

The day after the wedding, before Quiana could call her mother, the phone rang. It was her mother, Helen.

"Hi, Mom, I was just getting ready to call you. How are you, where are you, what are you doing, why did you call?"

"Quiana, stop! You know why I am calling you. Now, please stop with the small talk and tell me all about you and Minister Whitehead. I must say he sure seems interested in you. For a minute, I thought you and he were joined at the hip. You two sure looked good together. I think this is the perfect man for you! From the way, he was looking at you and trying to keep you all to himself, I wouldn't be surprised if within a year, he proposed to you."

"Mother, please, just stop! Don't go marrying me off to somebody I hardly even know. I just met him. Give me a chance to get to know him."

"Quiana, I know what I saw at Micaiah's wedding. Mark my word; this man is your husband. I have never felt this way about any other man you have dated. You are going to be Mrs. Stanley Whitehead. Have I ever tried to push you into a relationship with anybody? I always hoped you would find someone, someone nice, someone who would love you with his whole heart, someone who would be compatible to you; a man who adores you and would love you and protect you, a spiritual man. I see all those things in Minister Whitehead. And one more thing...I like him."

"I like him, too, Mom, I have been thinking about him all morning. Mom, I really, really like him."

———

The next day Quiana was still lost in her thoughts of the past when she heard her son call her. "Mom, will you please tell Paula to give me back my mp3 player?"

Quiana called out to her daughter. "Paula, will you stop picking on your brother? Please give back whatever you took from him."

Quiana had always wanted children, and God had blessed her and Stanley with twins. They were 13 years old and quite a hand full, but she wouldn't have it any other way. She and Stanley adored them. They were the sweetest kids, always got good grades and didn't mind helping around the house. They often would tell her and Stanley that they were the coolest parents, and how all their friends always wanted to come over to their house. Her children were her heart.

"Oh, God," Quiana thought. "I can't tell my children that I don't love their father. I can't let them know that I want to divorce him. I can't break up their happy home. My children are happy, they always have been."

She began to pray. "Heavenly Father, I come to you today asking for healing regarding my marriage. I am not happy in my marriage and not in love with my husband anymore. I know my husband loves me. He doesn't know how I feel. Please, Father, let your angels guide me. We have been married for 15 years and have two beautiful children. I thought we had the perfect relationship, we were so right for each other. I look back now and think maybe I should have never gotten married. I was 23 when we married; he was 33. I thought that he was perfect for me, and so did everybody else. Did I let others convince me to get married? 'Quiana,' they would say, 'what a man! Girl, I wish he was in love with me instead of you.' Even my mother told me, 'Quiana, I think this is the man God has placed into your life.' I was so overwhelmed by his charm. We so loved each other back then. What happened? Our minds are so different now than they were when we first met. Please, Lord, help me and help us. If only I could get back what we first had. There are times when I hurt so badly from wanting my husband to pay attention to me, to love me like he did when our love was young. Help me, Lord, to do the right thing, to do Your will—not my will, but Yours, Father. Amen."

Quiana always felt good after praying, she knew that God already knew her situation. She knew that by praying out to Him, He would listen to her heart and direct her path. She knew that He would answer her prayers in His time and He would give her guidance as to what to do. She remembered when she and Stanley would pray together all the time, but not lately.

The telephone rang. It was her mother, telling her she was in the neighborhood and asking if she was busy. Quiana worked from her home, her mother knew that she would always take time to talk to her and that Quiana welcomed her stopovers. "No, Mom, I am not busy. Come on over."

The doorbell rang. The twins ran to the door. "Mom, its Grammy."

"Well, open the door and let her in." Quiana thought her mother must have called from the driveway.

The twins loved their grandmother and she adored them. She spoiled them from the day they were born.

"How are my favorite grandchildren? Come see what I have for you." She handed them a bag containing two cell phones. They became so excited.

"Mom, look what Grammy gave us!"

Quiana turned to her mother. "Mom, I told them they couldn't have cell phones."

"Quiana, these phones are different, they are for emergency only. They are programmed so they can only call my cell, yours and Stanley's, home and 911. Please let them have them. God forbid if they needed to contact one of us due to an emergency and couldn't because they didn't have a cell phone. Almost every child their age has a cell phone."

Quiana stood there for a moment and looked at her mother. She was 60 years old, looked 49 and was always well dressed. Most people thought they were sisters. "Mother, you know how Stanley and I feel about them having cell phones."

"Please, Mom, please let us have them," Paula said. "We can only use them to call you, Dad and Grammy."

"And play games on them," their grandmother said.

"Please, Mom, please," said Paul.

"Oh, alright you can keep them, but you must do your chores and keep your grades up. If not, the phones are going back to Grammy Helen, is that understood?" The twins ran to their mother.

"Thanks, Mom. We promise we will do everything you said." And to their grandmother, running to hug her they said, "Thanks, Grammy, you are the best grandmother in the world, we love you so much."

"And I love you much more than that," their grandmother said.

Quiana had to look at her children and her mother. She loved the relationship they had. Paul and Paula were happy children. They thought their home was stable. What would happen to them if she divorced their father?

"Oh, God, please give me strength to deal with what I am feeling. I can't sacrifice my children's happiness for my own."

Helen stood looking at her daughter. "Quiana, I wasn't 'just in the neighborhood' today. I have noticed lately that you and Stanley seem to be a little distant with each other, not the madly in love couple you have always been. You know, I have never interfered in your marriage, and before I decided to come over, I asked God for guidance, whether I should speak to you about it. Do you want to talk about it? If you don't, I'll understand. I just want you to know that I am here if you need me."

With that, Quiana broke into tears. "Mother, I don't want the children to see me crying, please come into my office."

They walked into Quiana's office, closing the door behind them.

"Mother, I don't think I am in love with Stanley anymore and I want out of this marriage. I am so unhappy right now. I feel we are not a couple anymore. For ten years we were happy, everybody thought we were the perfect couple, and we were. But when he became pastor after Rev. Williams died, things started to change. We hardly talk to each other or do anything together besides going to church, and usually we take separate cars. We take special precautions to not let the children know we aren't getting along. And we haven't made love in months. What kind of marriage is that? We live together, sleep in the same bed and even will talk a little before we say good night. That's about it."

"This is not a home for me anymore, just a house we live in. Sometimes I look at him and I swear I hate him. Mother, please tell me how my husband can be a pastor of a large church where he counsels many couples about their marriages and can't fix his own. When I try to talk about what's wrong with us, he makes excuses and tells me we'll talk about it later, but later never comes. I can't live like this anymore. I'd rather take my kids and go."

"Quiana, what are you saying? Come, I want to tell you something. You know that your father and I have been married for 40 years. When we first met, I knew that he was going to be my husband, he was everything I wanted in a man and everything I needed a husband to be. We fell in love at first sight and within six months we were married. The first 15 years were great. We had you and bought a house. I went back to school got my B.A., then continued and got my M.A. I thought things were just fine, but what was happening was that both of us were too busy for the other and our marriage was being neglected. Where we used to always find time for each other, to eat together, to lay in bed and talk, holding each other and finding out how our day went, to be so totally wrapped up in each other was slipping away.

"We had the perfect family, the perfect relationship, I thought, but school got to be more important than family. Your grandfather became ill and your father decided he was giving up his principal job and take over his father's funeral business. I became so upset. 'Why can't one of your siblings take over the business?' I yelled at him, 'Every time anything happens, it's you who steps in!' He yelled back, 'I step in because I am happier with my family than I am with you!'

"We hardly ever saw each other. Then the complaints started. I was too busy to cook, too busy to take you to school. 'Could you please take Quiana to school?' I would almost demand of your father. We stopped going to church, just too busy and too tired. There was a lot of arguing and resentment. We were blaming each other for what was happening.

THE PERFECT RELATIONSHIP

"Finally, your father had had enough. One night he came home and told me he wanted a divorce; that he couldn't take it anymore. I was devastated. I asked what had I done, if there was another woman. He looked at me and I saw tears in his eyes. He said, 'Helen, I have loved you since the day I first saw you. I just can't live with you anymore. I want peace and happiness in my home. I want what we had when we were first married. Back then we loved each other so and were never too busy to talk. I have been trying to talk to you for months now and you can't find the time. I am seeing a lawyer before the week is over. You can have everything. I just want to always be a part of Quiana's life.'

"I didn't know what to do. I loved him and didn't want to lose him. I called your grandmother and told her everything. She told me that if I didn't want to lose my husband, I had better start putting my marriage first. She told me to start by putting God back in my life. I hadn't been to church in weeks, hadn't prayed either. I was too busy for God, but God wasn't too busy for me. This was a wakeup call for me. The next day I put everything on hold, I wasn't going to lose my husband. I went to the 12-noon prayer service. When Pastor Williams asked everyone to come up for special prayer, I was the first one to get up. After all, had left, I stayed behind. I went straight to the altar, got on my knees and asked God for help to save my marriage.

"Next, I went and spoke to Pastor Williams. I told him what was happening and that your father wanted a divorce. He told me that marriage is a committed partnership between a man and woman, and a challenge and that we should respond to each other's faults with mercy and patience. That marriage is a gift from God and we should try to save it.

"That is just what I did. I turned it all around. First, I told your father that I was sorry and to please forgive me. I told him

---

THE PERFECT RELATIONSHIP

"Finally, your father had had enough. One night he came home and told me he wanted a divorce; that he couldn't take it anymore. I was devastated. I asked what had I done, if there was another woman. He looked at me and I saw tears in his eyes. He said, 'Helen, I have loved you since the day I first saw you. I just can't live with you anymore. I want peace and happiness in my home. I want what we had when we were first married. Back then we loved each other so and were never too busy to talk. I have been trying to talk to you for months now and you can't find the time. I am seeing a lawyer before the week is over. You can have everything. I just want to always be a part of Quiana's life.'

"I didn't know what to do. I loved him and didn't want to lose him. I called your grandmother and told her everything. She told me that if I didn't want to lose my husband, I had better start putting my marriage first. She told me to start by putting God back in my life. I hadn't been to church in weeks, hadn't prayed either. I was too busy for God, but God wasn't too busy for me. This was a wakeup call for me. The next day I put everything on hold, I wasn't going to lose my husband. I went to the 12-noon prayer service. When Pastor Williams asked everyone to come up for special prayer, I was the first one to get up. After all, had left, I stayed behind. I went straight to the altar, got on my knees and asked God for help to save my marriage.

"Next, I went and spoke to Pastor Williams. I told him what was happening and that your father wanted a divorce. He told me that marriage is a committed partnership between a man and woman, and a challenge and that we should respond to each other's faults with mercy and patience. That marriage is a gift from God and we should try to save it.

"That is just what I did. I turned it all around. First, I told your father that I was sorry and to please forgive me. I told him

52 | P a g e

that I loved him and to please give us a chance to try and save our marriage. He admitted that he was just as much to blame as I was and that it wasn't entirely my fault. All he wanted to do was try and communicate to get back on track, but I had been putting him off, I was too busy. When he told me that, and when I stopped and thought about it, he was right. From that moment on, we both changed our attitudes. We put God first in our lives and turned to him for any situation we were facing. That was 25 years ago, and today, we are still very much in love.

"Quiana, I know what you have told me. I believe you still love your husband. I think you are unhappy right now with you both having busy schedules and not making the time for each other. We are always to look for reasons to restore the marriage relationship rather than excuses to leave it, and that is what I see you doing. You are unhappy and you would rather run than stay and fix it. I have never advised you on your marriage before, but you need to sit down and seriously think about if you really want a divorce.

"You and Stanley made a commitment to each other. As long as your marriage was fine, all was well; things start to go wrong, now you want to run. You think you don't love your husband any more. You think your marriage should be perfect? There are no perfect marriages, because there are no perfect people. Marriage is a challenge for both of you.

"Quiana, before you tell Stanley that you don't love him anymore and you want a divorce, think about what I've told you, marriage is stressful sometimes and complaining is a natural response. Pray, Quiana, and then pray some more. What's happening to you is what happens to a lot of marriages when they are neglected.

THE PERFECT RELATIONSHIP

"Look, it's the weekend. Why don't you and Stanley take some time off for the next two days, talk, renew your relationship and remember why you got married in the first place? I'll take the children home with me."

After her mother and the twins had left, Quiana sat down and thought about what her mother had said, "Remember why you got married in the first place." She thought of all the wonderful times she and Stanley had shared before they were married. She thought of the day he proposed to her.

———————

They had gone for a weekend in New York City. Stanley had planned the trip. The first day there, they had lunch at Sylvia's. Unbeknownst to Quiana, Stanley had hired a driver with horse and buggy to ride them through Central Park. It was waiting for them when they left the restaurant. She had always wanted to do that and had told him once how she would love it, that she thought it would be so romantic. He had remembered.

Halfway back, Stanley asked the driver to stop in front of the Conservatory Garden. When she heard that, her heart started to pound. They had gone there once when in New York on a business trip and had heard a young man proposing to his girlfriend. The scenery was so beautiful. Quiana was crying more than the bride to be. She had told Stanley that this was the most beautiful and the most romantic place for a couple to be when becoming engaged. He had remembered.

He took her by the hand, helped her out of the carriage and led her into the garden. When they were in the center, surrounded by the most beautiful flowers in the world, Stanley reached into his pocket and took out the most beautiful ring she had ever seen, knelt on one knee, looked into her eyes and started to speak.

DR. CAROLYN WHITE-BROWN

"Quiana, until now, I thought love was a mirage of the mind, an illusion, fake, impossible to find. But today, right now, I know that love is real and it exists. My love, I want to share my life with you forever. With you as my wife we can build, plan and work side-by-side as one. Right now, right here, I pledge my love to you. To take care of you and treat you right. I'll lie beside you each night and keep you warm and safe. I'll feed you and give you shelter. I'll help you and guide you and clear a path to protect you and shield you. I'll listen to your problems and help you solve them. I'll take your side even if you are wrong, just to prove my love. I'll plant you flowers and make them grow just to show how strong my love is. I'll whisper your name when you are far away from me. Because of how strong our love for each other is, you will hear it and know that we are one in heart. Quiana, will you marry me?"

"Oh God, Mother was right!" Quiana screamed. "How can I not love my husband? When I look back the past few months, it's been me. Yes, Lord, me, me, me. I have been so selfish. I have acted so foolish. When my husband became the pastor of our church, it kept him away from me often. I wanted him all to myself. I couldn't see it then, but I see it now. Even in the bedroom, I acted like a fool—turning away from him when he wanted me and wanting him when he was so tired that all he wanted to do was sleep. So, I gave up on sex all together, telling myself that he didn't love me anymore.

"Oh, Jesus, please help me. I've been so self-centered. I thought I had no one to talk to. Stanley is my pastor and I couldn't go to him as my pastor, but I could have gone to him as my husband. When I went to my friend Kima, she told me, 'Girl leave him! Just because he is a preacher man, that doesn't make him any different than any other man.' What a friend she was! Why didn't I go to Kayla? She would have helped me. And I should have gone to my mother instead of trying to keep it from her. Thank you, God, for giving me a wonderful mother who felt something was wrong and loved me enough to speak to me about it.

"When I think back to the day Stanley proposed to me, I was so in love with him. He was so gentle with his words. They were like a spark of light illuminating my soul. They brought a joy to my heart I had never known before—the sound of his voice, the way he touched my hand, the way his eyes lit up when he looked at me. I knew then that I loved him with all my heart.

"When Stanley came into my life, he brought light and music. I began to see and understand and taste the texture of true love for the first time. I asked God for true love and he sent me Stanley. I felt so fortunate that I had found a love so true that everyone dreams about. He made me happy, the way he would kiss me, sending chills down my spine. The way he spoke to me in sweet honesty and truth, his heart so caring. I was lost in his magic.

"Lord, I don't want a divorce; I don't want to lose my husband. I love him, but right now I am hurting so much, please tell me what to do. I am going to fight for my marriage and if all options run out, I am going to fight some more!" She burst into tears.

Quiana did not hear Stanley when he came home; she was crying uncontrollably. She was oblivious to her surroundings until she felt his arms around her, lifting her. "Quiana, honey, what's wrong, is it the children?" She couldn't stop crying. "Quiana what's wrong?" he asked again. "What is it?"

"Oh, Stanley, I have been such a fool. For the past several months, I have been so spiteful. I have neglected you and our marriage. I should have had the strength to talk to you about it. I wanted and needed you to know what was weighing on my heart. But when you come home, you seem to never have time for me anymore. Becoming the pastor of our church keeps you so busy. I needed to be your rock, your wife, your confidant, your lover. I wanted your attention and when I didn't get what I wanted, what I felt I needed, I became angry. I made up my mind that I didn't love you anymore.

"When you stopped kissing me when you left or when you came home, I said to myself, 'If he doesn't want to kiss me, then I won't kiss him, that'll show him.' You weren't making any sacrifices for me, or showing any affection. Yes, you took care of my practical needs, but what I wanted was a hug, a kiss, to hear you say, 'I love you.' In the beginning, you cherished every moment we had together. Now lately, you seem to have no time for me. I had made up my mind that we weren't in love anymore and I was going to ask you for a divorce. Then I remembered the day you proposed to me, the words you spoke, the way you made me feel. I loved you then and I love you now. I am willing to do anything to save our marriage. Please forgive me."

Stanley took Quiana's hand. "Come, honey, let's sit down. I want you to know that this is not all your fault. I am just as much to blame. When I took over the job as pastor, I became so involved. I was doing God's work and I thought you would understand. I didn't put in an effort to communicate with you. Instead of sitting together trying to reconnect, we both were too stubborn to see what we were doing to the other. When you came to me and wanted to talk, I turned my back on you. I was so busy preaching and counseling others, I forgot you, and I forgot us. I love you and the twins so much. You touched my life and made me who I am. You will never comprehend how you opened my heart to love and the wonders that love can do. I would never have let you divorce me. You are my will to live, an amazing person that fulfills every part of me. Before I knew you, I was nothing, now I am everything.

"Remember when we used to pray together, pray for each other? We took prayer out of our marriage. Here I am a preacher and too busy to pray with my wife, pray for my wife. I am so sorry I put you through this turmoil.

"Remember when we first got married, how we would sit and talk for long periods at a time and the love making was perfect, divine? We haven't made love in months. Here, I have a lovely wife who satisfied my every need and didn't wait for me to be the one to come over to her side of the bed all the time. I was so turned on by this. I was so much into my being a minister that when making love, I felt like we were sinning. It was so powerful and wonderful, the things we said and did to each other. I started to hold back from you. I would pray and ask God to forgive me. I thought it was wrong the way we carried on. I didn't know what to do. I didn't want to lose you. I would pray and ask God to show me what to do and He did. He directed me to the book of 1 Corinthians. It tells us that sex is a gift from God to married people for mutual enjoyment. Husbands and wives should not withhold themselves sexually from one another, but should fulfill each other's needs and desires. I wanted to come to you, but we had gotten so distant. When I came home, you would go into another room. As we lay down to sleep where we used to pray, you would turn on your side and sleep close to the edge not wanting me to touch you and when I would reach over and try to pull you to me, you would tell me how tired you were. And I would sometimes do the same to you. Our relationship was deteriorating. I didn't know what to do. I should have and I am so sorry for it all. Please forgive me. I love you and always will."

Quiana, looking at her husband with so much love, spoke softly to him. "We have done something tonight that we haven't done in a while. We have communicated. While marriage sometimes is conflicting and at times frustrating, we need to reach out to each other instead of turning our backs away from the situation. Love to me is like a flower, if you don't water it, nurture it, it will wither and die, it needs constant feeding. We had taken away the fertilizer from our marriage; there was no admiration. We had become selfish and had no gratitude.

"All our needs were being left unmet. Our marriage was deeply neglected. I was angry, depressed and resented you for it. But right now, sitting here beside you, feeling the love, I thought I had lost, I am so happy. I feel peaceful, safe and once more I am comfortable to be with you. I promise you that from now on I will come to you with any doubt I may have."

"Quiana, it is so good to have you back. I promise from this moment on to be open and speak honestly and sincerely with you about my feelings. I am so lucky to be married to you. Because of you my world has always been whole; you are my completeness, my eternal peace of mind. We have come together tonight as man and wife should, but we have left something out. If we want our marriage to be fruitful and thrive, we must put God back into it. Come, let us pray and thank our Lord and Savior for giving us this opportunity to renew our relationship."

Quiana and Stanley prayed together, taking turns.

Quiana began, "Heavenly Father, I come to You in the name of Jesus Christ to pray for my marriage. You said a house divided against itself cannot stand. I pray for unity in my home. I know this can only happen if we surrender and summit to You. I pray for myself and my husband to surrender all to You. You said that whatever we bind on earth in Jesus' name is bound in heaven and whatever we loose on earth in Jesus' name is loosed in heaven. I bind fear, intimidation, pride, rebellion, stubbornness, self-condemnation, self-righteousness, deception and rejection. Lord, I trust You for my marriage and ask You for Your continuous blessing upon it, my husband, my children and me. In Jesus' name. Amen."

Stanley then prayed, "We thank you, O God, for the love you have implanted in our hearts. May it always inspire us to be kind in our words, concerned for each other's needs and considerate of each other's feelings. Help us to be understanding and forgiving, strengthen us in our weaknesses and failings. Increase our faith and trust in You. Help us to focus on each other's strength and qualities and not the impurities. I praise You, Lord, for my marriage, that You have made us one in flesh and spirit. Thank You for opening our eyes and allowing us to see where You want us to be. Bless our marriage, O God, with peace and happiness; make our love fruitful and let there always be joy and peace in our home. Thank You, Lord, for my wife and children; You have entrusted them to me. Give me the strength to do Your will as a husband and father should. We love You, Lord. We give You praise, honor and glory. Amen."

Quiana hadn't felt this way in a long time. She and Stanley couldn't stop holding each other. It felt so good to touch each other like they used to. She had almost forgotten that the twins were not home and wouldn't be back for two days. She and Stanley were all alone. Before she could tell him, Stanley asked, "Where are Paul and Paula?"

"The children are with mom. She came over today and brought them cell phones. I was against them having the phones at first, but I gave in to it. I was planning on speaking to you about us giving them phones for Christmas. I hope you don't mind mom giving them the phones. You know how she spoils them."

"Mom had come over today to talk. She had sensed that something was wrong between you and me. I told her I was planning on asking you for a divorce. She told me to think about it before I told you. She told me to remember why I had gotten married in the first place and to remember my vows. She took the kids saying we needed to get away."

"Well!" Stanley shouted. "Let's go pack a bag! I know the perfect place. We can leave in the morning."

"But why?" Quiana asked. "We have the house to ourselves."

"Quiana, remember when we were first married, we used to pack up and go at any time. Let's be spontaneous. And Quiana, do you still have that red dress you wore to Micaiah and Calyiah's wedding? Please bring it. I love you in that dress."

"Stanley that dress is 16 years old. I only wore it once and was going to give it away, but you didn't want me to. I don't even know if it still fits, I've gained a little weight."

"Come, take off your clothes and let me look at you." She did as he asked.

Stanley looked at her with tears in his eyes. She was so lovely, and how close he had come to losing her. "Quiana, you are just as beautiful today as you were 16 years ago." He knew every curve of her body. "The dress will fit you perfectly."

As he led her into the bedroom, before he closed the door he spoke softly to her. "Quiana, until now I thought love was a mirage of the mind, an illusion, fake, impossible to find, but, today, right now, I know that love is real and it exists. My love, I want to share my life with you forever. With you as my wife we

THE PERFECT RELATIONSHIP

can build, plan and work side-by-side as one. Right now, right here, I pledge my love to you. To take care of you and treat you right. I'll lie beside you each night and keep you warm and safe. I'll feed you and give you shelter. I'll help you and guide you and clear a path to protect you and shield you. I'll listen to your problems and help you solve them. I'll take your side even if you are wrong, just to prove my love. I'll plant you flowers and make them grow just to show how strong my love is. I'll whisper your name when you are far away from me. Because of how strong our love for each other is, you will hear it and know that we are one in heart. Quiana, I am happy you are my wife."

"Oh, Stanley," Quiana whispered, "those are the words you spoke when you proposed to me."

Quiana recited a verse from her favorite poem:

"You are my lover, my dream come true
Forever and ever I will love you!"

Quiana and Stanley's problem was not being able to communicate with each other. In a relationship, you must be able to talk to each other, and not assume that the other doesn't want to be bothered with you because of what you are thinking and the reactions you are getting from them. They had become so busy in their everyday lives that they forgot each other. And they both were blaming each other for the problem when they both were at fault. They had removed all the time they had once shared in their relationship, they had no time to talk, to have fun, to make love. Their relationship wasn't a priority anymore.

When you can't communicate with each other, the relationship suffers. It can't grow. You start to resent each other— sometimes hate each other. This leads to separation and divorce. You may find someone else, but after a while, because you didn't learn how to communicate in your other relationship, the cycle starts all over again. Communication, I feel, is the key to happiness in any relationship. It helps the relationship to grow and helps you to trust each other.

By realizing what was missing from their relationship, Quiana and Stanley were able to save their marriage. They weren't perfect people, but were perfect for each other, the right partner for each other because they made themselves so. They completed each other because they had everything necessary that was wanted and needed by the other. Through it all, they stood by each other. When a couple stands by each other and stand together, they are unbreakable. What we have here is a perfect example of how an imperfect couple turned their imperfect relationship into a perfect one.

Chapter 3

Camille & Carol

When I first met Camille and Donald, who are both doctors, I thought they were made for each other. They seemed to be so much in love. But the difference between what you think sometimes about a couple's appearance in public and what is taking place in their relationship can be shocking.

About a year after I met Camille, she called me and asked if she could come over, that she wanted to talk to me about something. She was there before I could hang up the phone. It took her fifteen minutes to tell me what was on her mind.

"Kayla, since I've known you, I have come to really appreciate our friendship and I trust you more than anyone I know with what I am going to tell you.

"You know that Donald and I have been married for three years. I thought we had a great marriage, a perfect relationship, but we have a big problem and I don't know what to do about it. I am telling you this in confidence and please, please, promise me you will keep what I am going to tell you to yourself. I believe you will do as I ask. I can't go to anyone else but you with this, not my mother, sisters, no one but you. Please Kayla, tell me that you won't tell anyone. Promise me that, PLEASE."

I didn't know what to say at first. What could it be? Had she killed him? She said he was away for a medical conference, "Oh God. she is one of my best friends". I am going to trust her"

THE PERFECT RELATIONSHIP

I promise Camille, "I won't tell a soul. Now what is so horrible that you can't tell anyone but me?"

"Kayla, Donald is on the Down Low."

"Down Low! What is Down Low?"

"Kayla, you haven't heard about men and Down Low? Well, the term Down Low is used to describe the behavior of men who have sex with other men as well as women and who do not identify as gay or bisexual. They are referred to sometimes as being on the 'DL' or 'low low.' Girl, don't you watch Oprah? It was discussed on her show. She had some guy name King who had written a book about it."

"Camille, what are you saying? Donald is one good-looking Black man. I have even stared at him. You two make a very good-looking couple. And if he is what you are saying, why did he marry you? Why would he do that to you?"

"I didn't know he was when I married him. Anyway, remember last month when we had our monthly girlfriend's night out and I got sick and left early? Well, when I drove into my driveway, I saw the car of one of the doctors we work with, Doug, parked at the curb. He had been to our house several times, that's how I knew the car. When I think about it now, it was always when I was not there, usually on our girlfriend's night out. He would be leaving when I was coming home. I didn't pay any attention to it because he is a friend of Donald's.

"Camille, will you stop blabbering and tell me what's going on?"

"Well, when I walked into my house, something didn't seem right. I didn't see Donald or Doug. I looked in the family room, the living room; I looked all over. I decided to step out on the patio and there they were—having sex!

"Kayla, I heard them before I saw them and Donald was making more noise than he ever did with me. Well, I screamed and ran back into the house. I couldn't believe what I had just seen. How could he do this to me? Our sex life is wonderful; we have a loving relationship. I am sure he has been doing this for a long time. I am so angry. All sorts of things were going through my mind: what if he has AIDS, what if he gives me AIDS?"

"Camille, how did he explain this to you, what did he say?"

"Kayla, he told me he was sorry I had to find out the way I did, like he was going to tell me. I asked him why, that I thought he loved me. He looked me straight in the eyes and said. Baby, you know I love you. I love you with all my heart. You are my wife. I love you more than anything in the world. Now, Kayla, do I look like a fool? How can he love me and tell me he wants me to still be his wife?

"What's wrong with this picture? I walk in on him making love to a man and he says, "But baby, I love you, you are my wife" Well, not for long! I didn't go out looking for a man. I waited and waited until I thought I had found the right person. And when I thought I had, I went to the Lord with it. I wanted to make sure that Donald was the one. I prayed and asked God if he was the one. I was so careful with the relationship at first. I took my time getting to know Donald. I took a close look at who he was; I watched how he treated others and his family. I watched how he treated his mother and sisters. They adore him.

"What is it with me and the men I meet? I broke my engagement with someone else because he slapped me down for not being home when he came by. I knew he was coming over, I was cooking dinner for him, but I had forgotten to get the wine and went back out for it. When I returned, he was waiting for me. As soon as I got out the car, he hit me, asking me where I was coming from, saying that I was supposed to be home making dinner for him. I told him that I had forgotten the wine and went to get it. He called me a liar and asked me, 'Well, where is it?' I opened the back door, reached in took it out of the bag, hit him as hard as I could with it, ran to my door, took off the ring, threw it at him and told him the wedding was off and not to ever contact me again.

"I didn't date for a long time after that. I met Donald at a medical convention. He was such a charmer. It was six months before I went out with him. I liked him a lot, but I wanted to make sure that he was a good guy, someone who wouldn't try and take over my life, someone who wouldn't knock me around. I wanted the best; and I thought God was telling me that Donald was the one. Well, Donald is not the best, he's scum.

"When I look back, I remember things that happened that should have been a clue to this DL mess. He told me he and Doug had been friends since medical school. It turns my stomach to know that they have been doing this for a long time and God only knows with who else."

"Camille, does he use protection? Did you ask him?"

"I don't know, he told me he does, but I got tested anyway. I will get the results back next week

"You know, when I look in the mirror, I see a beautiful woman; intelligent, a doctor who thought she had the perfect life. I mean, a handsome intelligent husband who is also a doctor, nice home, nice cars and a little money in the bank. Nice friends, a good pastor and church home. What could be better? And I find my husband, the man of my dreams, having sex with a man.

"We are now sleeping in separate bedrooms, hardly speaking to each other. He apologizes to me every day. The other night, he came into my bedroom and asked if he could just lay in the bed with me, to hold me in his arms; that he just wanted to be near me. Well, I exploded and told him to get out of my room and out of my life. You know he broke down and cried like a baby. I had to get up and comfort him. He did what he did to me and here I am comforting him.

"Kayla, this man is playing me. Last week, I was doing my rounds at the hospital. I thought I had seen Donald go into a room. When I came to the room and looked in, it was empty; there was no patient in there. I was thinking where did he go?' I decided to look in the bathroom and there he was with another co-worker. I wonder how many more partners he has. I don't know what to do. That's why I need you. Please tell me what to do."

"Girl, I am at a lost for words. This is so new to me. I am your friend and here for you, but I am afraid you are going to have to solve this yourself. Why, I wouldn't even know where to start. There must be some type of program to help women like you. I will look into it if you want me to. But in the meantime, what about Donald? Does he know you saw him at the hospital?

"I am not sure and I don't care. I do know that tonight I am telling him he has to leave. The house is mine. I bought it before we were married and I don't want him there anymore. Can you imagine? Thinking you have this great relationship, the man of your dreams. He makes love to you beautifully, you are the happiest woman in the world and you walk in on him and another man.

"I can't stand to even look at him now. Today, at the hospital, he reached out to touch me and I pushed him away. Right now, I hate him and I don't want to be bothered with him."

When Camille got home that night, Donald was waiting for her. She walked right past him and went into her bedroom.

Donald called out to her. "Camille, we have to talk. Please."

68 | P a g e

She came back into the living room. "Yes, Donald, we do have to talk. I want you to pack your clothes and get out of my house. This marriage is over, as of right now, you are not my husband."

"Camille, please, I love you. You are the only woman I have ever loved. Let's work this out, baby, please; I don't want to lose you."

"Well, lucky me, how can you sit there and tell me you love me when you are sleeping with two men—or maybe there are more."

Donald looked a little shocked. "Two, what are you're talking about? Camille listen to me, the other night when you came home, I admit Doug and I were having sex, but it all happened so fast, I didn't know what to do. We had gone outside on the patio to smoke; you know you don't like it when I smoke in the house. He somehow came up to me and started to touch me. I pushed him back at first, but before I knew what was happening, he grabbed me and started to kiss me. I fought back, but he was too strong for me, the next thing I knew he was all over me. I still had on my scrubs. He pulled them down and the next thing I knew, we were having sex. Do you hear what I am saying? Sex, not making love. Not like with you, Camille. Baby, please, don't ruin our marriage by kicking me out, I love you."

Camille was so upset. "First, Donald, I said two because I saw you today at the hospital in the bathroom with another man. I saw you go into one of the rooms. I looked in and didn't see you. Wondering where you went, I looked into the bathroom and there you were. You were so busy you didn't hear me, and Donald, you were the aggressive one and you sit here and tell me lies. What you are telling me sounds like what a woman would say, 'He was too strong for me; I couldn't stop him.' Who do you think you are talking to? I am no fool! You sit there and tell me I am ruining our marriage. You moron, pack your things and get out—or do you want me to call the police to escort you? THIS IS MY HOUSE. GET OUT!

"I am going to see a lawyer tomorrow. I want a divorce as soon as possible and if you oppose it, I will tell everyone what is going on. Now get out!"

Camille ran over to where Donald was standing, reached up and slapped him again and again. He just let her do it. They both were crying.

The next day, Camille called and asked if I could come over right away. She was crying uncontrollably when I got there. She told me that Donald was gone; she had kicked him out. She was so depressed; she thought this man was her soul mate.

When friends and family would tease her about not being married, she would tell them that she was waiting on the Lord to place a man in her life, because He would give her the best. She had met Donald and had gone to God about him. She felt God was telling her that he was the one. They were so good together. Did God really tell her that he was the one or was it her?

When she looked back, she didn't think she rushed into the relationship, she waited awhile before going out with Donald. She wanted to get to know his personality; his friends, his family and everybody were so nice. She didn't see any signs of him being on the Down Low. There was nothing. But was it there all the time? God wouldn't have played this cruel joke on her; He wouldn't do that. He would not hurt her like this.

"Kayla, how do you really know if God is telling you something or whether you want something so badly that you say it's from God?"

"Camille, I think you need professional help with this one. If Pastor Williams were alive, I am sure he could give you answers. Now that Stanley is our pastor, you might not want to go to him, since he is married to Quiana and she is one of our closest friends. I am sure he won't disclose any information to her about you, but she is his wife, and husbands and wives do talk. I have gone to him with personal problems, and he has kept it confidential. But yours is way different. So, think about it."

"Kayla, you know I was thinking about getting together with Quiana and the others to discuss this. I mean if this happened to me, it could happen to anybody. Let's call everyone for a special meeting. I would like to know their opinions. Meanwhile, I am going to call and make an appointment to speak with Stanley. I like him as our pastor and I trust him to keep it confidential. I don't think he will mention it to Quiana unless I say it's okay for him to."

Camille had gotten an appointment to see Pastor Whitehead right away; she had gotten there early and was waiting for him when he came in. "Hi Stanley, I mean pastor."

"Hello, Camille, we have been friends for awhile now, it's okay to call me Stanley. I am still getting used to being called 'Pastor.' How can I help you? Are you and Donald doing okay?"

Camille started to cry. "My marriage is over. I asked Donald to leave, he has moved out."

"What? What has happened? You two seemed like the perfect couple. I counseled you before you were married. You spoke to me even before you brought Donald in. You wanted to make sure that he was the right one. You said that you felt God was telling you he was the one. What is it that now you feel that maybe you made a mistake, why did you ask Donald to leave?"

"Stanley, I came to you almost four years ago with the most wonderful news; that I had met the man of my dreams and I knew it was God who had placed him in my life. I wasn't out there looking for a husband. I wasn't searching. When Donald came into my life, I wanted to make sure he was the one. We were so compatible and could talk forever without boring each other. We liked the same things...and now I find out we really do like the same things."

"What are you talking about?" asked Pastor Whitehead.

"I just found out that Donald likes men. I came home last week and found him having sex with a man. Back when I came to you seeking advice, you told me to pray and God would give me my answer. You told me that if I wanted to be sure that Donald was the one God intended for me, to pray and God would let me know if he was the one. Well, I did what I was told, I prayed, I read God's Word; I asked for wisdom, I asked for guidance. Why didn't I see this? Donald and I are always together, we work together and we go on business trips together. I have never noticed him having an interest in men. Why didn't I see this? I prayed for us, I prayed for him. Donald said that he was praying for us also, that God was telling him that I was the one for him."

"Camille, I am so sorry for what you are going through. I feel that God didn't lie to you. When you came to me I told you to pray, especially when you were unsure of God's will for your life. I told you to be still before the Lord and wait patiently for Him. I gave you scripture to read, the book of James, which speaks of wisdom and patience and how He will guide our choices.

"The most important way God directs us is through His Word. God cares so much for us that He gave to us a guidebook, the Bible. We also have the Holy Spirit to recognize what is, or is not God's will for our lives. The Spirit of truth will guide you into all truth. Sometimes the Holy Spirit will either change our conscience if we're making a bad decision, or will soothe and give confidence when we're leaning toward the right decision. Even if God doesn't interfere, we can have confidence that He's always in charge. God can sometimes change a situation without us even realizing He has acted. The Lord will guide you always. We hear His voice when we pray, in Bible study and quiet thoughts of His Word. The more time we spend intimately with God and His Word, the easier it is to know His voice and His importance in our lives."

"Pastor, I am in so much pain right now. I just can't believe that I made the biggest mistake in my life by marrying Donald. I remember on our rehearsal day, this man that I caught Donald with was there. I was coming out of the lady's room and saw him and Donald embracing. I didn't think anything about it then, but when I look back I now remember them jumping and acting nervous when they saw me. Even after the wedding, Donald kissed this man on the cheek. Most of the other male guest he shook hands with, this one he kissed. I thought, 'Why is he kissing this man?' but I let it go, them being friends. I see so much now that I didn't see before. I should have paid attention to those little things. He was the perfect man for me, I thought. God was letting me see things and I wasn't paying attention to what God was telling me.

"The three of us went to a medical convention once. Donald and I weren't married then. He and this man shared a room. The next morning, I knocked on the door early because we all were going to jog before the meeting. I noticed that only one bed had been slept in and commented on it. This man said that he was up all night playing poker with some doctors down the hall and had just gotten in a few minutes before I did. I was a little suspicious, but I let it go. I wasn't paying attention.

THE PERFECT RELATIONSHIP

"I even remember my mother telling me to make sure that this man was the one, that just because I had known him for a while didn't mean that I really knew him. Now I wonder what she meant, did she know something? I think she would have told me if she had known that he was sleeping with men."

Camille thanked Pastor Whitehead for his time and went straight to her lawyer's office.

Meanwhile, Donald was on the job, he was thinking about Camille. Why did he do this to her? She was a kind and caring person. He was lucky to have her. He was on the Down Low long before he married her. He liked being with women and men. Now he had lost Camille. He would do anything to get her back, but he knew she would never come back to him. He had gotten himself into one big mess and he didn't know what to do but keep on doing what he was doing. His thoughts went back to the very first time he had contact with a man.

He was invited to a friend's house to watch the Super Bowl. When he asked if he could bring the girlfriend he had at the time, he was told that no women would be there. When he got there, it was a beautiful house; there were about ten men there. The food and drinks were plentiful. He started drinking, had a little too much and fell asleep on the couch. He woke up to one of the men kissing him and caressing him. He tried to push him off, but he was too drunk, and he was beginning to like what was being done to him.

At first, he was embarrassed, but when he looked around the room, most of the men had a partner. The owner of the house was an NFL player, a big, rough-looking guy. There was a schoolteacher, a lawyer, a construction worker, a CEO of a large firm (who was also a deacon in his church), a famous author, a professor from a nearby college, a lab technician, an assistant minister and another doctor, all professional men and all married except the NFL player, who was dating a famous model at the time.

"We all had beautiful women in our lives, some had kids and we weren't going to give that up. I continued to hang out with that group. It had become normal for me to get together with a guy; there were a lot of places you go to meet men like myself. And there were places you wouldn't believe you would meet brothers on the Down Low.

"I remember when I first met Camille; we had gone to church together. Before the service started, I noticed a well-dressed Black man had come in and sat in the pew in front of me. I knew he was on the Down Low the minute I saw him. He sat there during the service holding hands with the beautiful woman he had come in with. I found out after the service that she was his wife and that she was pregnant.

"Now how did I know he was on the Down Low? Well, before he sat down, he turned slightly, looked me right in my eyes and hurriedly licked his lips. That is something that Down Low brothers do to let you know they are DL. We who are DL know the signal. Those who aren't, never give it a second thought.

"At the end of the service, when Pastor Williams asked all to 'stand and greet your neighbor,' people got up out of their seats and walked over to people, shook their hands and gave them a hug. I was sitting on the end of my pew, when this brother got up, turned around and gave me a hug that lasted a little longer than it should. And, quicker than anyone could notice, he took his tongue and slightly licked my cheek. He did it so fast; I hardly felt it. On the way out, the aisle was crowded, and I slipped him my business card.

THE PERFECT RELATIONSHIP

When church was over, Camille made a joke of it by saying, 'The way that man hugged you, I thought I was going to have to pull him away from you. If that woman had not been with him, I would have sworn he was gay or something.' Little did she know that before the week was over, we were having sex.

"I didn't want to do anything to hurt Camille. When I met her, I thought she was the most beautiful woman I had ever seen. She was intelligent and was studying to become a doctor. We had so much in common. I just had to have her. I do love her and I don't want to lose her. I know she is divorcing me, but if I could, I would never leave her. She's a fantastic lover. I tried so hard to give up men when I met her, but there was always something to make me want to do it over and over again with a man. It's not like sex is better with a man; it's different.

"I will always love my wife and if she would forgive me I would go back to her in a heart beat. I would have to give up being on the Down Low. I couldn't live the lie anymore and you can't build a relationship on deception. That's why I am separated right now. But if I had told her in the beginning would she have married me?"

———————————

Camille had called a meeting at her house with their other friends. Camille wanted to know if any of them was in a similar situation or if they knew any men being on the Down Low. She was going to tell them what was going on with her; she didn't want them to hear it from someone else. These women were her friends.

When all were there, Camille had a hard time telling them why she had called the meeting. She told them that they were her closest friends and felt she could share anything with them.

DR. CAROLYN WHITE-BROWN

She went on to tell them that she was getting a divorce from Donald, that yes, she loved him, but she could not live with him anymore. She saw the puzzled looks on their faces.

"Ladies, this is hard for me to come forth with, but I love you all as if you were my sisters. I want you to know that Donald is on the Down Low; he has sex with men." They all were startled.

Briana was the first to speak up. "Wait a minute, Camille, what are you saying? Your husband seems to be all man, good looking and every woman's dream."

"You got that right," Kima said. "Girl, when I first saw Donald, I said to myself, "Damn, what a man, Camille sure is lucky to have him—and a doctor, too."

Marjorie, who is the most reserved of them all, spoke up. "Camille, are you sure? How do you know? Donald doesn't seem to be gay to me and he adores you, I can tell that he really loves you."

Camille spoke up. "I guess that since no one here has asked me what Down Low is, that you know about it."

"Everybody except me!" I blurted out. "Camille had to school me about it."

"Kayla, you are so naive. You need to get out more," said Kima.

"First, let's answer Marjorie's question. Remember last month when we were together and I got sick and left early? Well, when I got home, Doug's car was parked outside. You all have met Doug."

"Yes, we have, another hunk of man. And we all have met his girlfriend, Carol," said Kima.

"You mean his fiancé," Quiana added. "Did you see that ring on her finger? It's got to be at least eight carats. Where is she? I thought she was part of our group now. She is very nice."

"Ladies, I didn't think it would have been a good idea for Carol to be here right now. Anyway, I think she said she was going away on a business trip for two weeks," Camille stated.

"Why don't you want her here?" came a few replies.

"I was trying to tell you that last week—when I left you guys early—that when I got home, I walked in on Donald and Doug having sex."

Everyone was in shock.

"I felt something was wrong the minute I walked into the house; it was so quiet and Donald and Doug were nowhere in the house. I heard a noise on the patio, went out and that's when I saw them."

"What?" said Melody. "Who would have thought that these two absolutely gorgeous men would be on the Down Low? I thought men on the Down Low would look and act feminine, wear tight pants and be switching like women. Donald and Doug are good-looking men, masculine."

I had to add my two cents worth. "I can't believe that I was so ignorant about this. I didn't know too much about it until Camille told me. It's sort of scary, usually when there is infidelity in a male-female relationship, you think, "He's with another woman", now we have to worry if it's a man. I don't know what I would do if it was my Elijah. I am sorry Camille, but I don't think I could have done what you just did. Get it all out like that."

Kima commented, "Kayla, you don't know if Elijah is on the Down Low—as a matter of fact none of us know for sure if our man is, only Camille. And what about Carol, does she know Doug is gay?"

"Ladies," said Melody, "men who secretly have sex with other men while in a sexual relationship with women, do not consider themselves gay or bisexual, and they are so expert at hiding their secret lifestyle that the women in their lives have no idea they're cheating, much less cheating with another man."

Camille spoke up, "I am sure Carol doesn't know about Doug and we are not going to tell her, not right now anyway. I do feel sorry for her, but suppose we tell her and she doesn't believe us. She is head over heels in love with Doug. If we tell her and he says it's not true, who do you think she is going to believe? Their wedding is not until next year. We've got time to think of something. So please, when she is with us, please do not mention anything about this. But we are going to tell her before she marries that piece of garbage."

Marjorie went over to Camille and spoke gently. "Camille, is there anything I can do to comfort you? I don't know how you are feeling, but if it were me, I would be a mess."

"I am okay, I guess. I am glad I found out when I did. We have been married for almost four years, suppose it was ten or more years. I never saw this coming, not with Donald. I ask myself over and over, why did he marry me? I feel so used. He told me that he loves me and that since he was not cheating on me with a woman, it wasn't really cheating. Well, infidelity is infidelity, whether with a man or woman. The fact that he may have exposed me to AIDS devalues me as a woman. I feel so broken.

"I feel that Donald, being on the Down Low, prefers sex with a man he may have met for the first time than to have me. I feel that I am not worth too much to him. Not only is my marriage over, but it was a total lie. If this was going to happen, why couldn't it have been with a woman? I could come up with several reasons why he cheated. I could say our lovemaking wasn't good enough, I had gained too much weight, I had become unattractive to him, my housekeeping was bad, I was lazy and the list could go on and on. But that bastard had sex with a man in my house. The house we shared, he didn't even respect me enough to take it outside our home. Yeah, he loves me alright.

"I feel as though I want to beat up the other person. If it was a woman, I could confront her and slap her to make myself feel better. She and I could even get physical and roll around on the ground, but how do you get into it with a man? And this is a man I know and have known for a while. I want to tell Carol so bad right now, but I can't hurt her, I don't want her to feel like I am feeling right now. I saw Doug today, I wanted to tell all our co-workers about him and Donald, but that would be wrong."

"What would be so wrong about it?" asked Claudia. "I bet if Donald caught you having sex with one of us, he would tell everybody. You know men are different from women, you said yourself that Donald told you that since it was a man you caught him with that it wasn't cheating. But I bet if it was turned around, he would have beaten the mess out of you, that's what they do. Girl they will cheat around on you and act like you better like it and if you try to leave they will be all over you—and will kill you if you leave them. Edward thought I was seeing someone else and he put me in the hospital. No man wants their woman to leave them and it doesn't have to be for another man, either. Some are so mean, they will treat you like dirt, leave you with a bunch of children and pregnant with another baby in your belly."

"You are right about that, because that's exactly what happened to me!" exclaimed Kima.

Marjorie spoke up. "Ladies, right now we are concerned about Camille and Carol. And I don't feel that all men are as you say. I am not going to let you put my husband in that category. He is not like that. Some of us have had bad relationships and some are in bad relationships now. But when you say all men are cruel and malicious, that includes my husband and my husband is not like that at all. What if men put us all in one category? I think my Norman is one of a kind and not one of you is going to tell me differently."

"You go on, girl," yelled Kima. "Speak up for your man!"

"Camille, how do you know if a man is on the Down Low?" asked Claudia.

"To be honest, I don't know. If I did, I would have never married Donald. The other day I went on the Internet to find information about it. There is a lot out there. Some of it I believed and some I didn't. Because Down Low men are so clever at hiding their sexual orientation, it's not easy for women to sense it. A man on the Down Low looks just like any other man. He cannot be identified on the basis of how he looks. Contrary to popular opinion, Down Low men are not necessarily feminine looking. In fact, some of the most masculine, macho, manly-looking men are secretly sleeping with other men.

"When I look back, I did see things that Donald was doing. But it never crossed my mind that he was sleeping with men. He was my man; our life together was great. He used to look at women all the time; I didn't mind that. He would say, 'Isn't she pretty? But not as pretty as you!' Once, we saw this beautiful lady with the tiniest waist and he commented about it. Why would you think your husband is sleeping with men when he was always looking at women? Why would Donald deceive me like this? He could have slept with all the men he wanted as a single man. I just can't believe that this is happening. Married for three and a half years and now getting a divorce. I am happy we don't have any children. With all the trials and tribulations everyone goes through in a relationship, the last thing you want is a problem like this, and this is a big one."

I was about to speak when my cell phone rang. I looked at the caller ID; it was Carol. I answered on the third ring; all eyes were on me. The voice was almost hysterical, Hello Kayla, it's me Carol are you busy? No, I am not I will meet you in about fifteen minutes." I put the phone down, all were waiting to hear what was going on.

"What is it?" asked Camille.

"Carol is back and she wants me to meet her at Marie's restaurant. She didn't tell me why, but she was crying and told me to hurry. So, I will see you all later."

Camille said out loud, "I don't think we have to worry about telling Carol about Doug. I think she already knows."

———————

Carol was waiting at the front entrance. The minute I walked up, she burst out crying and fell into my arms.

"Carol, what's wrong, what happened?"

"Kayla, I didn't know who else to call. I know I just met you, but I feel that I can talk to you in confidence. I wanted to call Camille, but it would have been too awkward for me to speak to her, because it concerns Donald."

"Okay, Carol, stop crying and tell me what is going on, let's go in and sit down."

"No, I prefer we go and sit in one of our cars, if we go in there, someone might hear us and I don't want anybody to know about this."

We went and sat in my car.

"Kayla, I don't know how to start, this is hard for me. First, let me ask you something."

Kayla thought, "She sounds just like Camille when she called me. She has found out that Doug is on the Down Low."

DR. CAROLYN WHITE-BROWN

"Kayla, what do you know about men being on the Down Low?"

"Why do you ask?"

"Because I found out today that Doug is on the Down Low, he sleeps with men."

"How do you know that; did he tell you that?"

"No, he didn't tell me anything, he didn't have to. I have been away on a business trip for a week. I was supposed to be gone for two weeks, but I was able to do what had to be done a lot faster than I thought, so I flew back today. Well, anyway, Doug didn't know I was coming back early. I have a key to his house. I was going to relax there for a while and then have dinner prepared when he came home. I thought he would be at the hospital. I wanted to surprise him, but the surprise was on me. I thought it strange that his car was in the driveway, and even stranger when I saw Donald's car there, also. Anyway, they are friends, so I didn't think anything of it.

"I opened the door and went in. I didn't see or hear them, so I went out back to the pool and there was Doug and Donald in the pool naked, having sex. I was shocked. They were so busy that they didn't see me. I turned and ran back inside, went out the front door and called you. What am I going to do; I should have let them know I saw them. How am I going to discuss this with Doug? I know one thing—the engagement is off. And you know what; I am going to keep this damn ring. After what I just saw, I have earned it. And what about Camille? I can't tell her that Donald is on the Down Low. Kayla, please tell me what to do."

I didn't know what to do. "Excuse me a minute, I have to make a phone call." I got out of the car went over to the side and called Camille.

Carol couldn't believe that after what she had just told Kayla that she would dismiss it by making a phone call.

When I finished my call, I went over to the car, told Carol that I wanted her to follow me, that I was going to help her with her problem.

Unbeknownst to Carol, I had called Camille. I told Camille to keep everybody there, because I was bringing Carol back with me. That was all I said to Camille. I would let the two of them discuss it. I had to admit, this was going to be some day and I was right in the middle of it.

I pulled into Camille's driveway. Carol stopped at the curb and called out to me.

"Kayla, why are you bringing me here? What is going on?"

I got out of my car and went over to Carol's car and opened the door. "Come, the phone call I made was to Camille. She's waiting for us."

Carol went off! "Why did you bring me here? I can't face Camille! I should have called someone else! I thought I could trust you Kayla. I am leaving," and she started her car.

Carol was about to pull off when she heard Camille call out to her. "Carol, wait, please don't go, I know about Donald and Doug!"

Carol couldn't believe what she was hearing. "WHAT? You knew, you knew and you didn't tell me? I thought you two were my friends. I am leaving!"

"Carol, please, I just found out myself this week, I was going to tell you. I had to handle the situation with Donald and me first. Believe me, I would have never let you marry him without telling you. Please come inside, so we can discuss this."

Reluctantly, she went inside. She was again shocked to see the others. "What is going on?" she asked, "Why is everybody here?"

"Carol," Camille called out, "please, sit down and listen to me. We all are really your friends. I called everybody here today because I found out that Donald was having an affair, not with a woman, but a man. I think you know what I am going to say next. It is Doug, Carol. I know you know, because that is why you called Kayla, and the phone call she made while with you was to me."

Carol was furious. "So, all of you knew about this! All of you knew and not one of you told me. I am out of here; you all are not my friends."

Kima got up and went over to where Carol was standing. "Girl, sit your ass down and listen to what Camille is going to say. We are your friends and we are here for you. Camille only told Kayla about this first, the rest of us just found out today. We were going to tell you; we were just trying to figure out how and when. We knew you were away, but believe me we wouldn't have let you walk down the aisle with that scumbag. But girl, I will tell you one thing; you better keep that damn ring. What is it, about 8 carats?"

They all had to laugh at that.

Camille went over and hugged Carol. "Now that all my friends know about me, let's hear what you have to say and then we will work this out."

Carol started to cry. "I feel like a fool, why would Doug do this to me? I knew him for about five months before I went out with him. You know he chased me. I had just gotten the job I have. I am a pharmaceutical representative; I travel all over the country for the company I work for. It was on one of those trips that I met Doug, and when I think about that day, Donald was right there by his side. His lover was right there. I didn't even like him at first and ignored him. I came back here and ran into him at the hospital. He asked me out about six times before I gave up and went out with him.

"Ladies, tell me why a man who is secretly sleeping with another man would bring a woman into that. Doug could sleep with as many men as he wanted to. If he's on the Down Low, all he had to do was be himself. Why get married? Just be yourself.

"Why would a man who's on the Down Low pretend to be straight? There is never anything wrong with being who you are; nobody in the world should have to pretend to be something to lead a secret life. You think this is how they cover up what they are doing, by marrying and having girlfriends? They bring us into their world and when the mess hits the fan, we are the ones to get hurt; they go on with their lives.

"Camille, you say you walked in on Donald and Doug? Well then, what I just said is true; you caught him in the act with Doug and he goes on with his life. Today I walked in on them. They don't care about us. They are enjoying what they are doing.

"At first, I couldn't get my mind off what I had seen. This magnificent, attractive man, who I love so much, had lied to me, tricked me, misled me, conned me. The man of my dreams sleeps with men."

Camille spoke up. "Ladies the secret life of men on the Down Low is a mystery to us. None of us know if we are dating someone who is on the Down Low. It can surely prevent us from ever wanting to get into another relationship. I mean, after today and what I saw, how will I ever know if the man I am dating or married to isn't sleeping with his male friend he is hanging with? The way I am feeling right now, all men can go to hell!"

"Camille, I have to let Doug know that I know his secret. When I think about what I saw today, I get sick to my stomach.

Just thinking that this man I have been so intimate with was kissing and fondling a man. Why would he choose a man over me? Am I not enough, was I not sexually fulfilling? He told me once that he loved everything about me, that he couldn't wait for me to be his wife, that he wanted me to be the mother of his children and he wanted lots of them. I thought he really loved me, you know when we were out with his friends, he was always showing me off, 'Look at my baby, isn't she beautiful, isn't she this and isn't she that?' I was a showpiece, candy. He chose me for all the wrong reasons.

"He needed people to see him with me so he could keep his dirty little secret. How can I tell my family, my friends that my engagement is off? What do I tell them when they ask me why? He sure loves me, alright. I feel like going back over there and putting a little bit of Tae Kwon Do on his behind."

"Take me with you!" Kima yelled out. "I'll help you!"

"Carol it's going to be alright," Camille said. "We will work it out. Right now, we have to take care of ourselves. Did you and Doug use protection? If not, you need to go and get tested. Being a doctor, I tested myself. I would have been embarrassed to mention at the hospital that I needed to get tested for AIDS. When you are ready, I will help you, but you should get tested as soon as you can."

We all hugged each other and told Camille and Carol that we would be there for them if they needed us. Usually after one of our get-togethers, we would hold hands and say a prayer. This was no different, so Marjorie prayed.

"Heavenly Father, we come before You today in great need of prayer. Give us strength, Father, to forgive others who offend and wrong us, to excuse their transgressions against us and remove any persistent feelings of hatred. Let each trespass end as a closing chapter. Forgive our sins as we aim to forgive others. God of mercy, you know the secrets of all human hearts. For You know who is just and You forgive the regretful sinner. Hear our prayer, O Lord, and give us strength to go day to day forgiving, as You would want us to. We love You, Lord. Amen."

Carol stayed a little longer with Camille. She needed to talk with her more about what was going on.

"Camille, I don't know how you feel about this, but I am so angry. Why would our Black men want to deliberately hurt us like this? If they want to sleep with their men friends, why get into a relationship with us? I never saw this coming. I know I should confront Doug, but if I never saw him again in my life I could live with that. My problem is—what about the next relationship? You just don't know who to trust. You and Donald have been married for almost four years and you just found out. Don't they know that what they are doing is hurting us and could kill us, too? Black women have to be so careful, we don't know who we are dating and marrying."

"Carol, Black men aren't the only men that are doing this. It is not primarily a Black thing. It's an infidelity thing. But instead of the man cheating with a woman, it's with a man. The term Down Low originated in the Black community, but men of other races engage in this type of behavior, also.

"Down Low men come from all types of livelihoods. They are fathers, husbands, deacons, athletes, actors, lawyers, ministers, doctors—as we both know—and the list goes on and on. What about that governor in New Jersey? Imagine what his wife went through with that being so public.

"You know our young sisters, Black, white and others, don't have a clue as to who or what they will be dealing with when they start to date. Look at what happened to us. I don't know how many men Donald is sexual with; he put me at risk and Doug did the same to you."

"Camille, I am so happy to have you, Kayla and the others for my friends. I don't know what I would have done today if it hadn't been for all of you. I am going now, I have to find Doug and confront him with what I saw today. I want to hear what he has to say."

Camille walked Carol to her car and started back inside. Her phone began to ring just as she was entering her front door. It was Donald; he wanted to know if he could come over to pick up the last of his things. She really didn't want to see him, but she told him he could come, the things were packed and would be outside in the driveway.

After leaving Camille's house, Carol went home and phoned Doug to let him know she was back. He sounded happy to hear from her and asked her if she wanted to have dinner. She agreed and said she would meet him at Marie's at 7 p.m.

Doug was the first to get to the restaurant; he couldn't wait to see Carol. He was so much in love with her. She was such a lovely woman. He loved everything about her; even her name was perfect. He asked for a table near the door so he could see her when she came in. About five minutes later he saw her and stood up so she would see him. He thought to himself that something was wrong; usually when she saw him she hurried over and kissed him. Tonight, she was taking her time and she didn't look so happy, he thought maybe it was jet lag.

Carol wasn't in any hurry to greet Doug; all she could think about was what she had seen earlier in the pool. She was now standing at the table. Before he could help her with her chair, she had pulled it out herself and sat down. Doug leaned over to kiss her, but she turned her head away.

Doug was the first to speak. "Hi, baby, is something wrong? You look strange. How was your trip? I was surprised when you called me; I thought you were to be gone for two weeks."

"I was," she answered, "but things went a little faster this trip than usual, so I decided to come back early and spend some time with you." He didn't have a clue as to what was about to happen.

"Oh, by the way, I found your bracelet," he said. The clasp was broken; you must have lost it last week when you were over. I found it this afternoon and took it to have it fixed. Here it is."

She was glad he had found the bracelet; she didn't have to worry about how to start to tell him what she had seen.

"Doug, I didn't lose my bracelet last week, I dropped it today when I was at your house."

"Carol, what are you talking about? You weren't at my house today."

"I was there today. I have a key, remember? I wanted to surprise you. I was going to take a hot shower, relax and have dinner ready when you got home. I was surprised to see your car in the driveway, and Donald's." Doug wasn't saying a word; he had a look of total disbelief.

"I rang the bell. When you didn't hear it, I used my key and went in. I called out to you. When you didn't answer, I went looking for you. You were nowhere in the house. I went outside and I saw you Doug. I saw you and Donald in the pool having sex. I was shocked; I didn't know what to do so I ran. I hit my arm on the doorknob and that's when I broke my bracelet. I was in such a hurry to get out of there that I didn't stop to pick it up.

"Doug, why did you bring me into this? There is nothing more despicable than a Down Low man. Why? Because first and foremost, he is a liar. And Doug, you are a liar. You told me that you loved me and would never do anything to hurt me. You chased me down to go out with you. You knew you slept with men. Why did you need me? Was I a cover for you, so no one would know you are a Down Low brother? Well, don't just sit there looking like the cat that swallowed the canary. Say something!"

"Carol, please keep your voice down, people will hear. I love you. I want to marry you. I knew you were the woman for me as soon as I saw you. You are special to mé, so very special to me or I wouldn't have given you the ring and asked you to marry me. Do you know how much I paid for that ring? It cost forty-eight thousand dollars. That's how much I love you. I wanted you to have the best."

"Listen, Doug, don't tell me to keep my voice down! What's the matter; you don't want people to know your secret? Tell me, if you knew I was the woman for you the minute you saw me, was Donald the man for you the first time you saw him? You wanted me to have the best; well, Doug, you are not the best. You are an impostor and a fraud. It isn't bad enough that you are lying to me, your friends and your family—but you are lying to yourself. You choose to live a double life with me right in the middle of it. I didn't choose to be in a relationship where there is a third party involved, and the third party is a man and he is sleeping with my man.

"I trusted you. I still love you, but our engagement is off. I will not marry you. I didn't deserve this, but I do deserve this ring. You said it yourself, and I am going to keep it. And if you try to take it back, I will tell everybody in this restaurant and people we know that you are on the Down Low.

THE PERFECT RELATIONSHIP

"You know, Doug, I was looking forward to being a wife—your wife—and our relationship was great. I knew you loved me, but I didn't know you were loving someone else, also. Today, I was angry with you, very angry with you. You know at the end of the day we all want to be with someone who loves us, someone who makes us happy, makes us feel needed and gives us the attention we deserve; someone who we can trust in. You were that person for me. That is not a lot to ask for, we all deserve that.

"You have caused unnecessary pain and hurt for me, Doug. I didn't understand it at first. I asked myself why you did this to me! Once you met me, why did you continue to sleep with men? I know now that it has nothing to do with me and it is not a reflection on my femininity or my sexuality. It is all about you. I have no regrets about my relationship with you. If I hadn't found out about you today, I would have married you. I love you so, but please don't misunderstand my compassion. I am not excusing your decision to lie to me and put my life in danger. Next week I am going to be tested for AIDS, this is what you have done; put me in a situation where I could die. I don't know if Donald was your only partner, but whoever you were sleeping with, I was also. I pray that all will be well with the test. DAMN you, Doug."

Carol stood up. "I am not very hungry right now. I have to go. And Doug, one day you will be held accountable for your actions. Good bye, Doug."

When Carol got to the door she turned to look one last time at Doug. She could see the pain in his face. She felt sorry for him. As she walked to her car, she recited a verse from her favorite poem:

"And if we ever have to part
And go our separate ways

Memories of the love we shared
Will remain in my heart always!"

———————

Camille was in the kitchen making a sandwich; she thought she heard someone trying to get into her house. Then she heard a knock and Donald calling for her to open the door. She told him that she didn't want to see him and that he should take his things from the driveway and leave. He was very adamant and asked her to please open the door, that he wanted to see her. Reluctantly, she opened the door.

"Hi," he said, "I see you changed the locks. You look nice and smell nice, too. I brought you some flowers. Please take them; they are your favorites, yellow roses.

"Thanks," she took them and went to get the vase to put them in.

"Donald, you don't and will never live here again. I didn't want to ask you to give the keys back and I didn't trust you not to have duplicates made. I don't want you walking in here anytime you want. So, I called a locksmith and changed every lock."

"Camille, I want you to know that I am so sorry for what I've done to you. You were right; I should have never gotten married. I want you to know that I do love you; I love you with all my heart, always have and always will. You were perfect for me; whatever I wanted in a woman, you had. Please, let's not ruin the love we have for each other, I promise if you take me back, I will change. You won't have to worry about me being with men again. It's over I want you. I want my wife back. I love you so much."

"How can you say that? You cheated on me and with a man—as a matter of fact, two men. I caught you with two men. How many partners do you have Donald, are there more? Our marriage was one big lie. You did this to us, not me. I thought our marriage was solid. You broke it, Donald. Not me, you. All I wanted, all I needed in our marriage was truth and honesty. I feel as if I have been punched in the stomach, stabbed through the heart.

"The night I walked in on you and Doug I was in denial, I couldn't stop crying. The following days I was blaming myself, my self-esteem was down. 'How could he love me, but sleep with a man,' I asked myself. 'Was I not satisfying enough?' It was devastating; I was in complete shock. I felt so helpless. I had no one to turn to, Donald. I didn't want to, but finally I called Kayla and told her what had happened."

This was his chance to put the blame on Camille. "You know, Camille, you talk about my relationship with Doug. What about your relationship with Kayla and all your other friends? Every time something happens, you call Kayla or one of the others. What are their names? Oh yeah, Claudia, Quiana, Kima, Marjorie, Briana, Carol and let's not forget, good old Melody. I bet they have a lot to say. Are you sleeping with them? As far as I know, you all could be lesbians."

"Damn you, Donald, don't try and turn this around. You know what you are saying is not true. My friends are my friends, not my lovers. You know that. I've not been perfect in this marriage. I over spend; shop all the time, hardly ever cook and the house is a mess. But I didn't cheat on you. I was always faithful to you. I loved you and what hurts so bad is that I still do, but I can't live with you anymore. We had so much going on. I really loved our life together.

"When I met you, I went to speak with Pastor Whitehead. I wanted to be sure that it was all God's doing and not mine that had brought you into my life. I knew if it was God's doing, that I would have nothing but the best, because God don't give any junk. When I look back there were signs that you were on the Down Low. I wasn't listening to what God was telling me and I got junk. I know you are afraid to come out, but why choose to lead a double life? You jeopardized my life. We always had unprotected sex; you were my husband and there was no need to use protection. You should have been honest with me; I should have had an opportunity to make a conscious decision. I have heard that there are women who know their man is on the DL and still stay with them. If you had told me, I would have had an option. I wouldn't have married you, but at least I would have had that option. I want you to know that what you are doing is wrong. I have something I want to read to you."

She went and got her Bible. Before she read it to him, she told him that in no way was she trying to put him down, and what she was about to read to him were God's words not hers. She read:

"'You shall not lie with a male as a woman. It is an abomination.' (Leviticus18:22)

"'Do you not know that the unrighteous will not inherit the kingdom of God? Do not be deceived. Neither fornicators, nor idolaters, nor adulterers, nor homosexuals, nor sodomites.' (1Corinthians 6:9)

"I want you to know that I am not angry anymore. I forgive you. I hope we can be friends. I want you to know also that your secret is safe with me as long as I don't see you with any woman. Then, I will tell her about you. Not because I will be jealous that you are with another woman, but because I will be looking out for my sisters. Donald, I filed for divorce. You should be getting the papers any day now."

THE PERFECT RELATIONSHIP

She went over to where Donald was standing, put her arms around him and hugged him one last time. He was surprised that she was hugging him and so he held her tightly to him and whispered, "Baby, I do love you and I am so sorry. Please, please, we had the perfect relationship. We were made for each other and we loved each other so. Please, Camille, I don't want a divorce."

"Yes, Donald, we did love each other so, but no, we didn't have the perfect relationship. You and Doug do."

She pulled away, letting her robe fall to the floor. She knew he loved the way she looked; he was always telling her and always buying her bikinis to wear. She worked out daily to keep her figure.

"Donald, before you go, look at what you have lost." She walked over and opened the door. "Goodbye, Donald."

After Donald had gone, Camille thought out loud. "My marriage was excellent and I thank my Lord and savior for giving me the experience. I don't know why I was put in a situation like that, all I know is I had a man who loved me and I loved him back. I thought I was going to die when I found out Donald was on the Down Low, but to have had the love I had, I thank you, Lord, for that and I ask you, Lord, to open up Donald's eyes so he can see that what he is doing is wrong, and save his soul."

Camille went over to the vase of yellow roses, took the flowers out and threw them in the garbage. She then whispered a verse from her favorite poem:

"And if our love should ever stop.
I'll still not be alone. For I shall forever carry the love
You had for me imbedded deep in my soul!"

DR. CAROLYN WHITE-BROWN

Looking back at Camille and Donald's relationship, I would have to say that if Donald had not been on the Down Low, they could have had a good, lasting relationship. Camille told me she came into the relationship with complete honesty and openness. She trusted Donald to have done the same. She now knows that was not true. Theirs, she said, was the perfect relationship. When she looked into Donald's eyes, the way he treated her, loved her, she saw the perfect man, not that he was without faults, but he was perfect for her. Their marriage was fulfilling and happy.

Their relationship was good, Camille said, because they stayed focused on the present not the past and didn't worry about what could be. She said there was flexibility; that they were able to change or be changed according to the situation.

When I first met Camille, she told me that she and Donald both loved, honored, cherished and respected each other. They let each other know how much the other was appreciated. He would make her breakfast in bed, rub her back, massage her feet, clean the house and do the laundry. He was right for her and she him.

When Camille told others of her perfect relationship and they doubted her, she would tell them that a perfect relationship is perfect only to the ones that are in the relationship. If she and Donald thought that it was perfect for them, then who were others to criticize them?

But Donald being on the Down Low—how can you adapt to that? He lied; slept with men. She wasn't willing to compromise with that, she would never accept that. And so, the marriage was destroyed

Carol thought her and Doug's relationship was a good one. It took a while for Carol to go out with Doug. When she started dating Doug, she said that it must have been fate, or even God, because they had found each other at a time their hearts needed love the most. And when she got to know him, she knew he was the one. Then to find out that it was based on a lie? The man in her life that she loved with all her heart; she thought he had her best interest at heart and he didn't. She found out that he was self-centered, thinking only of himself. He betrayed her.

Relationships are all about trust. Trust to watch over you. Trust to take care of you. Trust to be able to rely on you, depend on you. Trust to open your heart to each other and know that the sky is the limit. How honest and truthful your connection is with each other depends on how well you trust one another to be who you are. You need that for the relationship to grow.

Honesty is always the best rule. You have to be honest with yourself and with your significant other. If Donald or Doug had told Camille or Carol about their secret, would the women have stayed with these Down Low men? Probably not, but they would have had the option to choose whether or not to get into a relationship with them.

Donald and Camille, Doug and Carol; four imperfect people who could have had the perfect relationship, if not for deceitfulness.

Chapter 4

Kima

Kima had been married to her husband, Albert, for eight years. They had four children, three of their own and one that Kima adopted that belonged to Albert and his mistress. I don't know if I could have taken my husband's love child into my home and raised him as Kima did. But we are all different and some of us will do what some of us won't. We all have to deal sometime with some difficult situations, but in the end, we survive.

The day I met Kima, I was walking to my bank, when I heard someone screaming for help. I stopped and looked towards the house that I heard the screams coming from. There was a little girl about seven years old, yelling for help. She was screaming that her mother was having a baby and needed help. She motioned for me to please come into the house. I really didn't want to go into the house; I didn't know if it was for real or if someone was using a child to falsely get me into the house. So, before I went in, I took out my cell phone and called 911, giving them the address and telling them that a woman was having a baby at home by herself. Once in the house, the child led me to where her mother was laying in labor; so much so that she couldn't get up. The contractions were about three minutes apart. I told the mother that I had called for help and they were on the way. I asked her if she wanted me to call her husband. She said she had and he told her that he was busy; to call 911 or her mother or somebody, that he didn't want to be bothered with that.

THE PERFECT RELATIONSHIP

I thought to myself, "What kind of husband is that to not come to his wife's aid, especially when she is having his baby?" She asked me to please help her, that she had two other children upstairs and needed someone to be with them until her mother could come. I asked if she had called her mother. She said she had tried, but the line was busy, and asked me to please try again, because she knew her husband would not come. I took the number and called her mother. On the fourth ring, her mother picked up. I explained the situation; she said she would hurry.

The emergency vehicle arrived, took over and was carrying her out the door on a stretcher just as her mother was running up the driveway. She asked her mother to stay with the kids and, to my surprise; she asked me if I would come with her. Now, I had just met this woman and I found myself getting into the emergency vehicle with her.

At the hospital, after her baby son was born, she asked me to again call her husband. I was shocked when he asked who the hell I was. He said that if she had me there, she didn't need him there and to please not call him again, that she was acting like she had never had a baby before. I told him that he was a piece of work and he should stop acting like a moron and take responsibility for his wife and newborn son. He cursed me out.

After the phone call to her husband, I went back to tell her what he had said. She started to cry, saying, "How did I ever fall for this man?" She asked me if I could stay for a while. She told me she was sorry that she had brought me into this. It was then that we realized we didn't know each other's name. She told me her name was Kima; I said I was Kayla. Once again, I thought to myself, Girl, what have you gotten yourself into"?

All I was doing was walking to the bank—which I never got to and now I was sitting in the hospital room of a woman I had only known for about two hours, who had just had a baby, and was telling me all about her life.

Kima was telling me how she had met her husband. "I was a graduate student when I met Albert. He had dropped out of college when he was twenty, said he could do well without a college education, had started his own real estate company and was doing pretty well."

"I was looking for an apartment and had seen an ad in the paper from his company and called. I wonder sometimes what my life would be like if I hadn't made that call. I met him to see the apartment and found out we had a lot in common. He was such a nice person. A gentleman; the perfect man."

"Our courtship was really quite wonderful. It wasn't until we were married and two babies later that I found out he was cheating on me and had a mistress that he had set up in an apartment. He would go on vacations with her while I stayed home with the children."

"He was so loving at home that I never suspected a thing. Then one day I got this call from a woman telling me she was sleeping with my husband and he was going to leave me and marry her. She said that she had been sleeping with him for a year. I didn't know what to say to her, so I hung up and called Albert. He assured me that it was not true and that he would never cheat on me, that he loved me and would never leave me. I believed him."

"For a few months after that, he was so attentive, so caring and stayed home more. He would play with the kids more and would tell me how much he loved me and his family; that he wouldn't know what to do if he lost us. Again, I believed him.

"Then one day my doorbell rang and this woman—I swear she looked like me—was standing there, handing me a baby boy that she tells me my husband is the father of. I knew she was telling the truth, because the baby looked just like him. She told me her name was Veronica and the baby's name was Albert Junior. She threw the baby at me. I had no choice but to catch him. Once I had that baby in my arms, she turned and ran back to her car and drove off. I went back into the house and called Albert. I hung up before he could question me. I wanted him home. He was there in no time.

"I was watching for him. The minute I saw him turn into the driveway, I went to the door with the baby in my arms. When he saw me, he knew right away what had happened. I could see it in his face. 'Whose baby is that?' he asked. 'Are you babysitting?"

"I said to him, 'Albert, I can tell by the expression on your face that you know that this baby is yours and Veronica's. How can you do this to me? Did you think I would never find out? When this woman called a few months back, you laid in our bed, making love to me and told me that she was lying, that she was an ex-employee that was coming on to you, that you ignored her sexual advances and she was now trying to break up your marriage. Well, tell me, Albert, how did she get this baby? And don't tell me he's not yours because, look at him, Albert, look at him; he looks just like you! In fact, he looks more like you than our two! Now you tell me, what is going on here? I trusted you, I believed you, I took you at your word, and now I am standing here with Albert Junior in my arms—and I don't mean our Albert Junior. How old is this baby, Albert? He looks to be about the same age as our Albert Junior. How old is he, Albert?'

"He looked at me and said, He is nine months old. He was born the day after Junior was born."

"Albert? He is the same age as our baby. How could you do this to me and how could you name him Albert Junior?' I walked over to him, handed him the baby and told him to take him back to his mother and pack his clothes and go, too; that our marriage was over.

"He took the baby out of my arms, put him in the play pen with our son and came over to where I was standing; took me in his arms and told me he loved me. He said he had made a mistake and had an affair with this woman for about a year, that he had always used protection. He went on to tell me that he had gotten tired of her and he didn't want to lose me; that he had told her it was over. After telling her this, she had invited him over to the apartment he let her live in; she had said for one last time to talk. Because she couldn't afford to have a place of her own she wanted to know if he would let her live there for a while to save for a place. He went over and since he had his own key, he let himself in. She came out of the bedroom naked, one thing led to another, they made love and the baby is the result of that night.

"I couldn't believe what I was hearing. I asked him, how can you say you love me? If that were true, then love should have brought you home that night. You stand here and tell me one lie after another. Get your baby and your lying, cheating self out of my house. How can you stand there and tell me you made love to another woman? You had love at home; you should have come home to me. If you really wanted to save our marriage, you should have come home to me. Now get out of here and stay the hell out of my life. I am divorcing you as soon as I can see a lawyer.'

"Before I knew what was happening, Albert rushed over to me and slapped me down."

"Who do you think you are talking to?' he said. "You are my wife; you aren't going anywhere. I pay the bills here, I take care of you and the kids, and you don't have to do one damn thing but look after the kids, the house and me. We are a family and a family we are going to stay. So, pull yourself together, go upstairs, clean yourself up and come back down like a good wife and we'll talk and decide what we are going to do with Junior Two, here."

"I went to speak, but he yelled at me, 'Woman I said get upstairs and clean up and then we'll talk!"

"I thought he was going to hit me again. I waited for it, and I was going to surprise him. When it didn't happen, I started upstairs. Half way up he yells, "Kima, take a bubble bath in the Victoria's Secret wash I brought you, put on that pretty red gown and put your hair down the way I like it. I am going to take care of the kids, feed them and get them ready for bed."

"I did as he asked. When I was finished, I went downstairs. He was waiting for me. The kids were all fed and in bed."

"He told me that he had called Veronica. She told him that since he had decided to stay with me, there was no reason for her to stay in town; that she didn't want to cause any more trouble, and she was going back home to Maryland. She couldn't take care of the baby, so she was leaving him with us. She told him that she knew I would take care of the baby even if I hated her. I couldn't believe he was telling me that his baby by another woman was going to live with us; that I was going to raise his mistress' baby.

"He looked at me and said, 'Kima, I am sorry I hit you, but I do love you. I love my family. I knew I had made a mistake the first time I slept with Veronica. Please forgive me and please say you will take care of the other Albert Junior. We have to keep him; he is mine. Veronica wasn't a good mother, anyway. She was always leaving him with strangers. She says she will sign papers to give us full custody of him. You are a perfect mother; you take care of our children beautifully. You may not love him now, but I know you, you will."

"I was furious 'Albert, I love my children; of course, I take good care of them. But how can you even ask me to take care of

DR. CAROLYN WHITE-BROWN

your lover's baby? And Albert, Veronica looks so much like me, I was shocked when I saw her; she could be my sister. Did that make it easy for you to sleep with her? Was she as good to you as I am, because I know I satisfy you and I know you love making love to me. I have to know, because I know there isn't a woman out there that could love you the way I can. When we are together, we give ourselves to each other so completely. I don't know about you, but I couldn't love anybody else the way I love you. I couldn't give myself to another the way I give myself to you. What was it Albert; why?'

He answered, "Kima, I said I was sorry. She looked so much like you that it was frightening. I guess that is what drew me to her. I knew it was wrong, but she looked so much like you I thought maybe she was like you in bed. I am sorry, but I had to find out. Anyway, she wasn't like you at all."

"Albert, you going to sit there and tell me that it took you a year to know that she wasn't like me? Please, I am no fool! Let me sleep on this and tomorrow, we will talk again."

"With that he became upset. He stood up, came over to where I was standing, looked me right in my eyes and said, "Kima, I have spoken. The baby stays with us. You are going to take care of him. As I have already said, we are a family and we are going to remain a family. Now shut up about it. I don't want to hear another word. Now get over here and take off that gown."

"Well, at that moment, I knew I had to speak up for myself. I yelled to him, 'Now, you listen to me. I am your wife, not your child. You aren't going to tell me to shut up—YOU are the one who messed up, therefore, you don't have the right to make the rules. Don't ever tell me to shut up again! And don't you ever put your hands on me again!'

THE PERFECT RELATIONSHIP

"He jumped up and drew his hand back to hit me. Before he could, I grabbed him and flipped him over. I kicked his butt all over the room. He didn't know. I had trained at Tiger Schulman before I met him and was still a member. I went to training every week. He might have hit me once, but damn if he was going to put his hands on me again, ever. I helped him to get up; he tried to hit me again. Before he knew what was happening, I was all over him. He was down again and tried to get up, but I gave him a karate kick that sent him backward into the fireplace. I thought I had better have a little talk with him.

"Albert, I don't want to hurt you and I can, so please don't ever try to hit me again. You caught me off guard earlier, but that won't happen again. I can defend myself, so please don't make me hurt you.' I started toward him. He must have thought I was going to hit him again; he put his hands up in front of him to protect himself.

"Girl, I was going to beat the living daylights out of him. I began to talk to him. 'As of right now I am going to tell you what I want and the first thing is to go to bed. I have had enough for one day. We can talk in the morning. And Albert, you can sleep on the sofa. In fact, I don't care where you sleep, as long as it's not with me. Now, get up, clean yourself up, and Albert, why don't you put on some of that Victoria Secret cologne for men that I bought for you? Good night!'

"The next day, I was up early; I had three children to take care of, two of them under a year old. I wanted to have time to think things out before they woke up. It was hard enough taking care of my own children and now there was one that wasn't even mine. But, I couldn't take it out on the child.

"As I sat there, I knew that my marriage would never be the same. We were already having problems in our marriage. I knew

Albert was cheating on me, but I wasn't sure until I got the call; and even then, with the lies he told me, I wanted to believe him. I wanted to save our marriage. What was I going to do? Thank God, I had gone to school and had something to fall back on. After getting pregnant with Brooke, I went on maternity leave. We decided that while I was home, we would have another baby and Albert Junior was born. I did not go back to work; we decided I would stay home and raise our children. Albert said that he could take care of everything and that is what he did. I have to admit, he took very good care of us; his real estate company is one of the biggest in the state. You see the house we live in, it's gorgeous and the neighborhood is beautiful. Kayla, where do you live?"

"I live one block from you. I love the neighborhood, also. I have been there for fifteen years. My husband and I had been searching for a house for about three months when we found it. We knew the minute we saw ours that it was for us."

"Kayla, I know I just met you, but I feel I have known you for a while. I feel so comfortable talking to you. Do you mind if I go on? I feel I have to get this out; I can't talk to my mother about this. She feels that I have a good husband and should forgive him. My father cheated on my mother, he was abusive to her, but since he took care of her and us, she let him, telling my brother and me that he was a good man, that if it wasn't for him, we wouldn't have the nice things we had. I made up my mind right then that I would not let a man abuse me. And I meant it. I didn't want to hurt Albert, but when he hit me, I knew I had to protect myself. If I hadn't shown him I could defend myself, he would have continued to hit me. Once a hitter, always a hitter. You should have seen his face when I flipped him. He was in total shock!"

THE PERFECT RELATIONSHIP

"Kima, tell me why you are still with this man. I am listening to all you are saying, but you are still living with your husband and are having his baby…or is it?"

"Yes, I am, and yes, it is his baby and I am going to continue to live with him until I am finished with my plans. You see, I couldn't leave; everything was in Albert's name until several months ago. I have no money. When we got married, I had ten thousand dollars in my account. Since then, I have managed to add another ten thousand dollars. I have four kids to raise, all under the age of ten. If I divorce my husband, twenty thousand dollars will not last long. I want my children to have a nice home in a nice neighborhood, like where I live now; they all are going to college. I want to go back to school. I was just getting ready to go back to law school when I met and married Albert."

"Kima, I don't want to get all up in your business, especially since I just met you today, but since you feel you have to tell me all about your life and I must admit that it is interesting, tell me why did you get pregnant—and are you saying that you are going to raise another woman's baby after you leave your husband?"

"First, for a while after the mess had hit the fan, Albert was so good to me. After he found out that he couldn't push me around, for a while he was a very good husband, he treated me well. I thought everything was going to be alright, so we made love and the result is my new baby son Todd. He told me that he wanted to make sure that I and the kids were well taken care of, so he had my name put on all his legal papers and business accounts. Like I said, that was several months ago. I know that he has a very big project that he is working on and in three months he is going to profit over ten million dollars. I intend to get half of what he has and I am going to try and remain in the house. I hope I don't sound like a monster to you, but you don't know what I have been going through."

"Well, I guess you are going to tell me."

She laughed. "This is the first time I have been able to speak out like this. I don't have any friends. I told you about my mother, and my brother Ian, who lives in California. We talk often, but I don't tell him what's going on between Albert and me. If I did, I know he would come and confront him. He hated the way our father treated our mom. He told me if Albert ever put his hands on me, he would have to come and straighten him out. I can handle Albert myself.

"And yes, I am going to raise the child of my husband and his mistress. I have adopted him. I am his mother now. I feel that he didn't ask to be in this mess, and I have come to love him. I feel he is just as much mine now as my own children are. I did legally have his name changed, though. It is now Isaiah. I wasn't going to have two Albert Juniors!

"Kayla, I hope I am not keeping you from anything, but please stay a little longer."

I was now so engrossed in the conversation that I didn't want to leave. "Please," I told her, "Go on." And she did.

"Well, after I got pregnant with Todd, Albert changed. He became argumentative. The least thing would set him off and he would leave. I knew something was wrong, that he was starting the arguments to get out of the house. I knew he had to be cheating. To be honest with you, I didn't give a rat's ass if he was cheating. I had made up my mind what I was going to do. This only made it more so.

"I would play with him. When he would try to start an argument, I would not say a word. He would get so frustrated with me. When I wouldn't give him what he wanted, he would start to call me names, bad names. I still wouldn't argue with him. He would start cursing and yelling at me and when I wouldn't respond, he would tell me that he couldn't take it anymore and leave.

"Unbeknownst to Albert, I had hired a private detective to follow him. If I was going to divorce him, I needed proof that he was having an affair. If I was going to take him to the cleaners and get what I wanted, I needed something substantial for court.

"Now I hope you don't think that I am one of those women whose husband has cheated on her and now she is going to get revenge, you know, a scorned woman. I am just making sure that my kids and I are going to be taken care of."

Kima went on to tell me that she and her husband have no relationship at all, that he acts like he hates her and sleeps in the spare bedroom. He doesn't help her with the kids, and all during the pregnancy he had treated her badly. She said that once, she got herself and the kids all dressed up to go out for dinner, it was Mother's Day. He told her that he wasn't taking her anywhere and he left. Her mother told her the next day that she thought she had seen them, had yell out to them, but it wasn't her; he was with another woman and that the woman looked like her.

"Kayla, when I heard that, I knew what was going on. Albert had never stopped seeing Veronica. I was raising their child and they were probably laughing at me. But I was going to be the one to have the last laugh."

It was getting late and I really had to go. I told Kima that if she'd like, I would come back in the morning. I really wanted to come back, not just because her story was interesting, but because I liked her and wanted her to know I would be there, if she needed me.

DR. CAROLYN WHITE-BROWN

The next day, I went to the bank and hurried to the hospital to see Kima. As I was rushing into the hospital, I bumped into a young woman who, for a moment, I thought was Kima. I spoke to her.

"Excuse me, but you look so familiar, I feel as though I know you. Have we met? Is your name Nancy?" That was my way of getting her name.

"No, she answered, my name is Veronica."

Well, I couldn't believe it! Why was she here? Then this tall, dark, sort of good-looking man got off the elevator and called out to her, "Veronica, over here."

Well, damn, it had to be Albert, and he was with his girlfriend. Wow, the nerve of him bringing his girlfriend to the hospital with him—and his wife just had a baby! "Come on girl, it's none of your business, and make sure you keep this to yourself," I told myself. I took the elevator upstairs and headed straight to Kima's room. She was feeding the baby when I walked in.

"Hi, how are you this morning?"

"Kayla, I am so happy to see you. I really didn't think you would come back after all that I told you yesterday. You won't believe what just happened. Albert was here. He said he wanted to come to see the baby and to tell me that he wouldn't be home when I came home; he has to be away for two weeks. He told me that the project he was working on had come through sooner than he had thought and that he had to go to Maryland. Well, the minute he said Maryland, I knew he was going to be with Veronica. Like I told you yesterday, I really don't care, because I know what my plans are; I just thought he would see that the baby and I got home first. When I asked him about that, he said to me, 'Why don't you ask your mother or your friend that called me yesterday to come and get you.' He went into his wallet, gave me a thousand dollars and told me that it should be enough for me to get home and get some things for the baby. I tried to explain to him that I needed a baby seat and some clothes for the baby to wear home. He told me he had to go, that he was on his way to the airport and he left.

"Kayla, how can he be so cold towards the baby? If he doesn't care about me, at least take care of the baby. Will you help me? My mother is with Brooke, Isaiah and Albert Junior. I will tell you one thing; Albert is going to be one sorry man when I am finished with him. He doesn't know who he is fooling with. I am asking God to forgive me right now, because when I finish with him, he won't have a pot to piss in. And one more thing, I swear I smelled the perfume that Veronica was wearing when she came over and threw Isaiah in my arms. He smelled like he had just given her a hug or something."

I didn't say a word.

The next day, I took Kima and baby Todd home from the hospital. Kima was a little sad at first; she kept remembering what it was like when she and Albert had taken Brooke and Albert Junior home from the hospital. This time, if it wasn't for me, she would have been all alone. I felt a little sorry for her to have to go through nine months of being pregnant alone. I can't even imagine going through that alone.

Kima and I got to be very good friends. I introduced her to the others and they all liked her very much. We all took turns babysitting for her when she needed it.

By now, Albert had moved out. He told Kima he was going to give her six months to get a job. He told her that he would take care of the kids, but she could take care of herself. Albert was living with Veronica. She was a cold one, and she never once came to see her son.

Kima said she had run into Veronica and Albert downtown once. She asked Veronica if she wanted to see a picture of Isaiah and Veronica replied, "Why? He's yours; I don't want to see him." Kima said she wanted to strangle her. She didn't understand how Albert could become involved with a woman as cold as Veronica and believe every lie she told him. Veronica was calling Kima almost daily and telling her that Albert was divorcing her and was going to kick her out of the house. When Kima would tell Albert, he would tell her that she was the one who was lying and she was jealous of Veronica because she was a younger version of her.

Well, Albert was going to be in for a great awakening, because Kima was now ready to go ahead with her plans. She had a lawyer; in fact, her lawyer was Marjorie. Yes, Marjorie is the quietest of us all, more reserved, but when it comes to her job, she is one shrewd female.

Albert's ten-million-dollar deal had come through right after Kima had come home from the hospital. Thank God for her friend who worked at the firm. She had called to congratulate her, not knowing that Albert hadn't said a word to her about it being completed.

Before Kima could call Marjorie to tell her that it was time, she received a certified letter from Albert's lawyer. Albert had filed for divorce. Kima called Marjorie. Marjorie told her that she would take care of it. She called Albert's lawyer and an appointment was made for all parties to come together.

Kima had given Marjorie a lot of information that she thought would surely be good for her case. She was sure she was going to get what she wanted. She didn't want to hurt Albert; she just wanted to make sure that she got what she felt rightfully belonged to her and the children.

The day of the hearing had finally arrived. There they were, sitting there with their lawyers. Kima was thinking, "Lord, I always thought that when I got married that it would be forever." She looked over at Albert, he seemed to be sad also, but he was the one who had done this. She had given Marjorie all the proof she hoped would get her what she wanted.

Albert's lawyer spoke first. "Divorce to me is a bittersweet moment, because it is the death of a marriage. A couple gets married, loving each other dearly, and then before you know it, here we are. My client here tells me that he was willing to save the marriage, but your client was not. Since she did not want to reconcile this is what we are proposing. Now Mrs. Jackson, Mr. Jackson is giving you full custody of the children. I understand there are four. He will give you five hundred thousand dollars cash and two thousand dollars a month for child support until the youngest child is eighteen. There are two houses and one condo. Mr. Jackson feels that since he bought all three, that they rightfully belong to him, but you can remain in the one you are living in. But when the youngest child is eighteen, you will have to vacate the property. Now Mr. Jackson feels that this is more than enough, and he also wants visitation with the children, under an agreement mutually satisfactory to both."

Kima was about to speak, but Marjorie whispered to her and told her that she would handle Mr. Cohen.

"Mr. Cohen, does Mrs. Jackson here or I look like a fool? Did you come in here thinking that I would let my client take what you just offered? Absolutely not! Do you know that your client is worth a little over ten million dollars? And you sit here and want to give my client a measly five hundred thousand cash and two thousand dollars a month until the youngest child is eighteen? What about college for all the children? You mentioned that there are four children. Did your client tell you that only three of them belong to Mrs. Jackson and the one that she adopted belongs to Mr. Jackson and his mistress? My client has had the child since he was nine months old."

"Now Mr. Cohen, very sadly, more than half the marriages in this country today end up in divorce. Couples today are breaking their marriage vows like no tomorrow. Instead of 'for better or for worse; for richer or for poorer; in sickness and in health; forsaking all others; until death do us part,' it's 'now until somebody I like better comes along.' And that, Mr. Cohen, is what happened to my client. She did not ask for this divorce as you stated she did—as a matter of fact it was my client who tried to save the marriage. When his mistress had the baby, Mrs. Jackson forgave Mr. Jackson and even adopted the baby. He continued to cheat, and walked out on her. He was abusive, both verbally and physically. And with all that he has done, he wants to give his wife who was always faithful to him, crumbs. Well, I think not, Mr. Cohen. After what my client has gone through, this is what we are putting on the table…

"Half of the business; she will take five million dollars and her name comes off all papers pertaining to anything Mr. Jackson owns. Of the three properties, she will keep the one she is now living in; your client will sign it over to her and pay all back taxes on it, if any. She is okay with having full custody of all the children. The visitation, as stated, is okay with my client. My client will get seven thousand dollars a month until all four children have finished college."

Albert jumped up. "Now do you think I am crazy? The business is mine; I had it before we were married! I am not going to give you half of it, and besides, your name is not on it. You are doing this because I left you for a younger woman."

Albert's lawyer looked through his files and pulled out a document and slid it over to Marjorie. "I am sorry, but what did you say your name is?"

Marjorie looked at him, feeling a little annoyed. "It's Marjorie, Marjorie White."

Mr. Cohen looked up at her and said loudly. "Marjorie White, I've heard about you. You have quite a reputation. You are a fighter."

"Mr. Cohen, I am sure that you fight for your clients just as much as I fight for mine, now what is this paper?"

"Look at it he said, my client thought your client would come up with something like this to get half of his business. Her name is not on these papers."

Marjorie went into her files and slid over to Mr. Cohen an exact copy of the document. "Well, her name is on this one. I went with her to the bank myself to get it. I had a court officer with me and the bank manager also was there when the box was opened. He is a notary. Here are statements from all parties' present and they have been notarized, stating that her signature is on it. You see, we thought your client might try to pull something like this."

Albert jumped up again. "When did you go to the bank to get this?"

"It doesn't matter when I got it. I knew you would try this. I told you I am no fool. I have to admit, I felt like one and you treated me like one. Remember the day you came to the hospital, the day after Todd was born? I smelled Veronica's perfume all over you. I knew it was hers, because she was wearing it when she came and gave me her son. Well, when you left, I looked out the window and I saw her with you leaving. I was so hurt; I didn't tell anybody about it, I didn't want anyone to know that my husband wouldn't even come to the hospital to pick up his wife and new baby boy, that he had his girlfriend with him when he told me he wouldn't be picking me up. I knew you would try and find a way for me not to get what is rightfully mine. I remember when we first got married, you insisted that I come with you and have my name put on the business. You said that if anything happened to you, I would have the business to support me and the children we would have together. Well, something has happened and I am going to make sure our children and Isaiah are taken care of. Several months ago, you had me put my name on the bank accounts and more business papers. And Albert, I didn't touch one dime, probably because I knew there was nothing much to touch, but now there is.

"All of this is on you; you wanted Veronica. Well, you can have her, and if you don't give me what I want," she reached in her bag and pulled out a handful of pictures, "I have these to show to Veronica and the judge."

Marjorie intervened. "Mr. Cohen," she said, handing him the pictures, "these photos will show that your client didn't just have an affair with the mother of the son that his wife is now caring for, but with two other women, as well. My client has been married to Mr. Jackson for almost ten years. She has been faithful to him; she has loved him like no other. She didn't want this divorce, she stated that. But why would she stay married to somebody who is going to cheat on her and be unfaithful? She has to get out while she can! Once a cheater; always will be a cheater. My client now wants the divorce. She feels she deserves everything we are asking for here today. If your client won't agree, we can go to court and let a judge decide. Here is my card, where you can reach me." Marjorie and Kima got up and left.

Kima cried all the way home. "How could I have been so stupid? When I first met Albert, he was a charmer. I thought I had found the perfect man. How could he treat me like he is now? And the nerve of him to tell me I was angry because he left me for a younger woman! Veronica is three years older than me. I checked her out, and she is lying to him; doing to him what he is doing to me. I wonder if he knows she was arrested for shop lifting, imagine that."

"Kima," Marjorie asked, "how do you know all this?"

"I hired a private investigator. I feel so bad, to think I did that to check up on Albert and Veronica. I guess when you are angry you will do anything. Marjorie, do you think he will give me what I am asking? I feel I deserve every penny. I just hope Veronica doesn't retaliate and want Isaiah back. I love him as if he were my own. I know she doesn't want him. I have tried several times to have her come see him; she won't. Why wouldn't a mother want to see her child? He is a beautiful little boy. What will I tell him when he grows up?"

"Kima, you will tell him the truth. And if he wants to see her, let him. She is the loser here. Let her be the one in pain then. I must tell you, I don't know if I could have taken in my husband's love child."

When Marjorie got home, her phone was ringing. It was Mr. Cohen. He told her that Albert would give Kima what she wanted, that he wanted to get this over with as soon as possible, because he and Veronica wanted to get married. Marjorie couldn't believe what she was hearing; she called Kima and told her the news.

It had been two years since the divorce. Kima is happy with her children and is in law school. She never thought she would feel this happy again. Albert doesn't cross her mind. All the mess he put her through is far behind her.

Her thoughts were interrupted by the doorbell ringing.

Kima opened the door and Albert almost fell in. She had to use all her strength to keep him from falling. She helped him inside. "Albert, what is the matter; are you sick?" He tried to answer her, but passed out. Kima rushed to the phone and called 911.

She called Kayla from the hospital. She was hysterical. "Kayla, please, I need you! Please come to the hospital. Albert is here, he passed out at my house!"

"I am on my way, where are the kids?"

"The kids are with Mom."

When I got to the hospital, Kima was a mess; she rushed into my arms crying. "Kayla, they say it is bad, he had a heart attack and he might not make it. I couldn't contact Veronica.

"I was surprised to see him at my door. He looked so sick. When he passed out, I thought he was dead. I thought something was wrong two weeks ago when he came to see the kids. He usually takes them with him; but he told me he wasn't feeling well and asked if he could just visit with them. He stayed so long, I didn't think he was going home, and he was especially nice to me. Finally, I asked him to leave. I told him that the kids had to go to bed, and even then, he asked if he could tuck them in. I knew something was wrong.

"Later, Brooke told me that she didn't want to go over to his home anymore, because Veronica is always arguing with him and that he is the one who takes care of them when they are there."

A doctor interrupted their conversation. "Mrs. Jackson, I am Dr. Woods, your husband is in serious condition. He had a heart attack and a stroke. He is paralyzed on the left side. He will make it, but he will need around-the-clock care. He will be here for a while. When he is well enough, we will send him to a rehab facility. There, he will be given therapy for his paralysis. I will be his doctor while he is here; here is my card, feel free to call anytime."

"Doctor, I am not Mrs. Jackson—not anymore, we are divorced. I don't know where his wife is. I am only here because he came to me; he was at my house when this happened."

"Well, you need to find her right away, let her know what has happened. Mr. Jackson needs his family right now." With that he walked away.

"Kayla, I can't believe this. I can't do this. I shouldn't even be here. Why did Albert come to me if he knew he was sick? He could have come here to the hospital. What is going on? I am going to see if I can see him. Then I will call my mother to see if she can keep the kids for another day, and then I am going to find Veronica."

On the way to Albert's house, Kima thought about what had transpired the day before. Albert always picked up the kids on Friday and kept them until Sunday. When he didn't call, she called his house and then his office. His secretary said that he had called and said he wasn't feeling well and wouldn't be in all weekend.

"Why didn't he call me and say he was sick?" she wondered out loud. She pulled into his driveway. Veronica's car was there.

Kima took out her cell phone and called Albert's house number. On the third ring, a man picked up.

"Hello, may I speak to Veronica, please?" Kima asked. The man told her to hold on a minute. Veronica picked up.

"Hello?"

"Veronica, this is Kima, I am in your driveway, please come outside."

"What do you want? I am not coming out there for you to jump me. Get off my property!"

"Veronica, Albert is in the hospital, he had a heart attack and a stroke, and you need to get to the hospital right away."

"I have done my job," Kima thought to herself after she got back into her car. She was about to back out of the driveway when Veronica came out. And behind her came a man that looked like he was high on drugs.

"What did you say, Albert is in the hospital?" "Yes, you need to go there."

"Kima, you were there with him?"

"Yes, he was at my house when it happened."

"Then, Kima, if he was at your house when it happened, you take care of him. You go to the hospital, I am busy. This morning, when he told me he was having pains in his chest, I told him to go to the hospital, not your house. Now if you will excuse me, I am busy. Goodbye."

"Veronica!" I screamed, "What is going on? You wanted Albert so badly—now you act like you don't care about him! He's your husband!"

"No, sweetie, he's your husband. Albert didn't marry me. After the divorce, he shut down on me, telling me he had made a mistake; that he loved you and you would always be his wife. He told me I could stay in this house, but he won't put it in my name. I found his will; this house is in your name. If anything happens to him, you are his beneficiary. I am not his wife; I am not going to the hospital. I don't give a damn about him. Now, please leave me the hell alone...and one more thing, Kima. I want my damn son back. I have relatives; they can raise him." Veronica turned her back and walked away.

Kima almost lost it. She knew she had to be calm, but that statement got to her. "Isaiah is my son and she will never have him." As she pulled out of Albert's driveway, she continued talking to herself, "Damn you Albert; damn you."

Kima called Marjorie and told her what was going on. She told her that she didn't want to be responsible for Albert, but she wanted to know if anything happened to Albert, if Veronica could get Isaiah back. She made an appointment to meet with Marjorie at the law firm.

The following morning, before meeting with Marjorie, Kima went to the hospital to see Albert. She was surprised to see him looking so well. He was just as surprised to see her; he didn't think she would come back. She told him about Veronica not coming; she didn't get into details, but he knew. He asked Kima if she would come and sit closer; that he wanted to talk to her. She did as he asked.

"Kima, I am so sorry for what I put you through, the awful way I treated you. I feel God is punishing me now for all the mean things I did to you. Veronica wasn't worth it. She will never measure up to you. Please forgive me. I put you through hell and here you are looking after me. I want you to know that I never married Veronica. I was going to, but the day after our divorce was final, I came home and caught her with a man in my house. I knew right then that I had made a mistake. She told me some lie, hoping I would believe her. But I knew the truth, just like you did when I was lying to you."

"Albert, right now I am concerned about you getting better. Have you talked to Dr. Woods today? What did he say?"

"Yes, he was here earlier. He told me that I had a heart attack and a stroke. He wanted to know what was stressing me out. I told him where I am right now in my life. Next week, I am going to a nursing home rehab to start therapy. I can't use my right arm. Kima, will you help me through this? I know Veronica won't come. She did call and she told me that when I get out of the hospital, I can find someplace else to live. That she has already packed all of my things and she is sending them to your house."

Before Kima could think, she snapped. "That stupid woman; I thought I was through with her!

"Albert, I am sorry. Yes, I will see you through this. Now if you will excuse me, I have to meet with Marjorie. Before I go, I would like to ask you two questions. First, why didn't you tell me that you never married Veronica and second, why am I your beneficiary? Veronica told me all this when I went over to your house; I wanted her to know what was going on with you. She told me everything. She also told me that she wants Isaiah back, that she has relatives that can raise him. I want you to know Albert, that even though Veronica is Isaiah's biological mother, he is my son. I am his mother. I will never let her have him. I should have known you really didn't love her, or you wouldn't have had an affair with those two other women."

"Kima, I am such a fool, Veronica was young."

"STOP, right there Albert—she is three years older than me! If you wanted younger, you had that at home. Yes, she lied about her age."

"She was fun," he snapped. "After you had Brooke and Albert Junior, you spent more time with them than me. I wanted your attention. There was no passion or romance in our marriage anymore. You didn't have time for me. It was all about the kids."

"They were babies, Albert! They needed my attention. All you had to do was be patient, talk to me and tell me what was bothering you. I always came to you; I wanted you to open to me. You shut down Albert; there was no communication. And then you cheated on me and lied about it. You took the trust out of our marriage. I loved you, Albert; I really loved you. But I don't want to talk about that now. That part of our lives is over. Let's concentrate on helping you get better. Just one more thing, Veronica told me that the house she is living in is in my name. Is that true? If it is, I want to see the papers."

Albert didn't seem too upset about Kima having that information. "Yes, it is. After what I found out about Veronica's past, I made sure that if anything happened to me, she wouldn't get anything. Everything I own will be left to you and the kids. I even put in my will that I am Isaiah's father and he is to remain with you, that Veronica is not a fit mother; that she threw him away. All this information is in my office in my safe. If you want, you can look at the papers. Do you remember the combination? I didn't change it; I wanted you to have access to it if anything happened to me."

"Albert, one more thing. I know that you are going to be alright. I just want your permission to do one thing that is going to solve our problem."

"Of course, what is it?"

"I am going to get rid of Veronica; I am going to kick her out of my house."

Albert nodded his head, "Thank you."

After Kima left, Albert cried. He realized he had messed up. He wondered why he ever left Kima. She was perfect for him.

Kima met with Marjorie and told her what was happening. The first thing she wanted to do was make sure Veronica couldn't get Isaiah back. Once that was taken care of Kima was going to kick her out of the house and out of the state and their lives forever.

The next few days, Kima took care of Albert. She made sure that he was comfortable in rehab and doing what was necessary to improve his health so he could come home. Then, it was time to confront Veronica.

A certified letter had been sent to Veronica telling her she had to vacate the premises. Kima had given her more than enough time to get out. Now the fun was about to begin. Kima pulled into the driveway with the City Marshal behind her. She almost ran to the door. The Marshal had to call out to her to wait; he had to be the one to tell Veronica to vacate the premises.

"Well, come on and do it!" Kima yelled.

The Marshal rang the bell. When Veronica came to the door, she demanded to know what he wanted and why Kima was there. She started to scream at Kima, telling her to leave. Kima was ready to pull her out, but the Marshall stopped her.

"Are you Miss Lee, Miss Veronica Lee?"

"Yes, and who the hell are you?"

"Miss Lee, I am Mr. St. John, from the City Marshal's Office. We sent you a notice to vacate these premises a week ago. The notice was sent to you certified, and an eviction notice was taped on this door. We have a return notice with your signature that you did receive these papers. I am here today with the owner of the property, Mrs. Jackson, to make sure you leave today. Now please step aside, I have people here with me who will be moving all of your belongings out."

Well, Veronica went off! She had forgotten what she had told Kima.

THE PERFECT RELATIONSHIP

"This house belongs to my husband and he has given me the right to live here as long as I want! And if you all don't leave right now, I am going to call the police and have you thrown in jail!"

Kima spoke up. "Veronica, I hate to tell you this—no, I love telling you this: this house is mine, it's in my name and you don't have a husband. Albert was smart enough not to marry your sorry behind. Here is the deed to this house, its mine; now you get your junk and get the hell off my property before I call the police and have you thrown in jail."

"You can't talk to me like that. I am going to call Albert right now and he will tell you."

"Call Albert, you haven't spoken to Albert since he's been in the hospital. You haven't seen him and you don't care about him. All you care about is yourself. Now get out of my house!"

Veronica shot back at Kima, "You wait; I'll show you! Albert left you for me and you are just jealous! Me, he chose me, a younger woman, not your old, worn out self."

"Veronica, you are three years older than I am, so you are the old hag here! Yes, Albert left me for you, but he knows now he made a big mistake. That's why he wouldn't marry you; he knew you were the scum of the earth. Now get out of the way so these men can get your junk out of my house."

"Kima, you will be sorry for this, you just wait. And I want my son back! I had him, he came from my womb and his name is Albert Junior, not Isaiah."

Kima was very calm. "I was waiting for you to bring that up. Yes, you are Isaiah's biological mother. You gave birth to him, but he is not your son, he is mine and you will never get him back and now let me tell you why. You stand there and tell me that you are his mother; well, a mother who loves her baby would never have done what you did. When you were pregnant with my baby, you never had prenatal care. You told Albert that it wasn't needed, that you didn't have the time to go see any doctor. Two weeks after he was born, you gave him away to strangers, people you had just met. Albert told you he was going to have you arrested if you didn't bring him back. Albert wanted so much to put you out; he was so ashamed of what he had done to me. He told me that he used to come and sit outside my house with Isaiah in his arms. He took care of him until the day you brought him to me. You threw that baby in my arms like you would a ball, and you never looked back; even when I tried to get you to look at a picture of him, you wouldn't and now you stand there and tell me he is your son? Isaiah—yes, his name is Isaiah—is MY SON and if you think that you can get him back, then you just try it. The courts will have a field day with you.

"When he is older, I will tell him he is adopted—and only then. He can make up his mind if he wants to see you, but right now you stay the hell away from my son. He's MY SON. Now one more time, move out of the way so these men can do their job. I want this house empty as soon as possible so I can fumigate it."

Veronica was yelling and screaming, "You can't do this! Where am I going?"

Kima yelled back. "I don't care where you go! Try hell!" For a moment, she felt sorry for Veronica. But she knew the Bible does say that you reap what you sow.

Albert was in rehab for eight weeks; Kima went to visit him every day. When it was time for him to come home, Albert asked Kima to forgive him for the way he had treated her and to please take him back; that he still loved her. That he knew even when they were sitting at the divorce table that he loved her, but he

THE PERFECT RELATIONSHIP

didn't know what to say to her to get her back. He wanted his family back and would do anything to make it right again.

"Please, Kima," he begged, "I want to come home. I know you love me, because if you didn't, you wouldn't have done what you did and you wouldn't be here with me now."

Kima got up and stood by Albert's bedside. She took his hand, "Albert, the first time I saw you, I knew that we were meant to be and I knew that you knew it, also. When our love was young, we were inseparable, we loved each other so. To us, we had the perfect relationship.

"When the babies came, you became selfish, you wanted all my time. Babies can't take care of themselves. But instead of you being a good father and husband, you went and found someone who would give you all the attention that you weren't getting at home. You even picked someone who looked like me, hoping she would do all the things for you that I wasn't doing at home. I tried to talk to you, but you wouldn't listen. I would call you at work and tell you to come home, that the kids were napping and we could have had a few minutes to ourselves. At night, I would have the kids in bed early. Take a nice bubble bath and have on your favorite body wash and sexy gown. But when you came into the bedroom, you would look at me and then go sleep in the guest room. Once, I even came to you in the guest room and you turned me away. How much of that could I take? You would look at me like I disgusted you. Yet you slept with dirty Veronica.

"I was raising our family and you didn't have the patience to be patient. You began an affair and even had a child—a child that you had the nerve to name Albert Junior, knowing that you already had a Junior at home, a child that you demanded I take care of. You abused me, both verbally and physically. You divorced me, Albert, for a slut and you wanted to give me peanuts. You divorced me for someone who was using you and didn't care a damn about you; someone who left you to die in the hospital; someone who never came to visit you, to see how you were doing; someone who thought that if anything happened to you, she would somehow get something; someone who threw you to the curb when you needed her most. You say you love me? No, Albert, you don't. Relationships are what make us human and a marriage is one of the most special relationships we can have. You ruined our marriage, Albert."

Albert started to speak, "I know I made a horrible mistake, but I want my family back. You mean so much to me. We are human; we all make mistakes, but I have learned. I've changed and I can improve. Through this, I believe we can change our relationship and live for the better. I know we can change this divorce into a relationship where, once again, love can blossom. Please, Kima, say you will be my wife again. We had a good marriage."

"Yes Albert, our marriage used to be good, but you changed all that. You see, in a good marriage a husband and wife respect each other and avoid temptations of infidelity. In good marriages, husbands and wives are generally nice to one another, working together as a team. When problems occur, the husband and wife communicate and try to fix it.

"When the kids came along—kids that you wanted—you couldn't deal with the change and you left us. You walked out like it was nothing; you didn't care about us. You didn't just walk out and leave me and my kids, but you left your mistress' child with me, also. And now, when you feel you have made a mistake, you want to kiss me, tell me you love me and I am supposed to run into your arms and open my doors and my legs back to you. No, Albert, I can't do that. Maybe another woman could, but I can't; I won't. I loved you, Albert, but you stole the most precious part of our marriage by sharing your body and experiencing someone else's.

"Albert, I do love you; you are the father of my four beautiful children. But I am not in love with you. We can never go back to being man and wife. I am happy with my life right now. I love my children, school is good, and thanks to you, my financial situation is great. There was a time when I envisioned you coming back to me. I didn't know what to do. I didn't know how to survive the pain. I was spending all my time in denial, hoping for your return. But I got through the bad times. I had the children to consider, so I moved on; I accepted the reality of it all. You know that everyone who goes into a marriage believes it will last forever. If they didn't believe, then why would they bother? Most of us believe in fairy tales, at least once. You took my fairy tale and turned it into a nightmare.

"Right now, I am happy. I have forgiven you for what you did to our family. There was a time when I was so angry. But I had to give that up; I am now free from all that thanks to my dear friend, Kayla, and all the other friends I met through her. I am okay. I survived; I am a survivor.

"Albert, you can't force a relationship and be happy in it. And you can't come back to a place that you once loved and expect it to have all that it once gave you.

"I saw Dr. Woods downstairs when I was coming in; he is discharging you tomorrow. I will be here to take you home. I fixed up the house you and Veronica shared. It looks nice. Everything is brand new. I have hired a nurse that will be living with you for as long as you need her.

"You know Albert; I have asked God to forgive me for not taking you back. When we said our vows, it said for better or worse, in sickness and in health, till death do us part. My vows tell

me I should take you back, but knowing that you slept with someone like Veronica, knowing that she was sleeping with other men while sleeping with you, makes my skin crawl. I can never give myself to you again as a wife is supposed to."
Kima bent down and kissed Albert on the lips. "I will see you in the morning. Goodbye, Albert."
When Kima was in her car, she took a minute to think back. "When we were courting, and later as newlyweds, I felt my marriage would never have any problems—any major ones, anyway. I assumed that we would always be as passionate as we were back then. I thought our marriage would be a good one forever. Any marriage takes work and a lot of couples can work it out if they work together. Albert didn't want to work with me to save it, and I couldn't do it by myself."
Kima started to cry. And then she recited a verse from her favorite poem:

"And if we ever have to part
And go our separate ways
Memories of the love we shared
Will remain in my heart always!"

When the kids came along, Albert was jealous of all the time Kima spent with them and was feeling left out, even though it was Albert who wanted to have children. He should have told Kima how he felt when the kids came along. Some men want all their wives' attention. Albert wasn't mature enough to know that kids need to be taken care of.

THE PERFECT RELATIONSHIP

Kima thought Albert was the right man for her when she first met him. Before they had children, their marriage, she thought, was a good one. They had planned their kids; they were emotionally and financially ready.

In a marriage or any relationship, you go through changes. As their household changed, Albert became impatient. He didn't have his wife to himself anymore. There was a lack of communication. He should have told Kima his feelings. Instead, he started an affair, hoping to satisfy his selfish needs, but only making things worse.

Their relationship became abusive. The marriage was already deteriorating. There is no recipe for transforming a weak relationship into a restorative one—and having an affair is not the answer. Its takes teamwork to heal from infidelity and both husband and wife must be willing to commit to it. Could this marriage have been saved? Maybe, with counseling. What would you have done.

Chapter 5

Marjorie

Marjorie and Norman have been married for ten years. They have two beautiful children, Norman, Jr. and Taylor. Marjorie is a lawyer and Norman is an inspector for the sanitation department. When he and Marjorie met, he was a garbage collector.

Once we became friends and she told me this, I wondered how they met. Usually when you are a lawyer, the men you date are either lawyers or someone from your circle of friends. Now, I am not trying to put Norman down, because he is intelligent and a fine-looking man—an amazing man—and he really loves Marjorie. He married her within a year and he treats her like a queen. But how does a garbage collector get a beautiful woman who is in law school to marry him in less than a year? You won't believe her story.

———————

Marjorie told me she met Norman one day while she was walking to get the bus and he was collecting garbage. He told her that she was one fine-looking woman and asked her out on a date. She told him not in a million years and hurried on her way. About two days later, she was late putting her garbage out. She ran out to catch the truck, and who would be in the truck but Norman!

Once again, he tried to get her to go out with him and once again she refused. He looked a mess, dirty and smelly.

THE PERFECT RELATIONSHIP

Marjorie was in her last year of law school; she thought she could do better than a man who collected garbage. The men she dated were all in college, and one was already a lawyer. She thought the garbage man must have been crazy to think that she would go out with him. She couldn't even stand to talk to him. Go out with him? Please!

But Norman would not give up. On her garbage pick up days, he would always spend a little longer on her street, hoping to see her, and if he didn't see her, he would leave two dozen red roses at her door. Once when she came home, she found her front porch full of roses, they were everywhere.

Marjorie had to tell him to please stop all the things he was doing because she would never go out with him, and if he didn't stop, she was going to have to let his job know that he was harassing her. She even went as far as to tell him that he wasn't her type and she had no interest in him whatsoever.

Norman was a little upset at what Marjorie had told him. He knew that this lovely woman was indeed going to be his wife, and within a year. He just had to take another approach.

He had asked a neighbor about her one day, and the neighbor had told him that she was in law school and that he didn't have a chance in hell of getting her to go out with him. Well, Norman was going to see about that! He was thinking, also, that Marjorie probably thought that he wasn't educated enough for her, not good enough for her; that he couldn't take care of her. Well, he was going to show her—and later, he would tease her about it after they were married.

"I am going to show this woman that she is going to be my wife and the mother of my children," he thought to himself. And so, he put his plans in motion. He wanted to show her that if a man loves a woman, really loves a woman, that he would do anything to please her. And please her he would, and please her he did.

Norman and my Elijah are so much alike. Sometimes when Marjorie and I are talking about our husbands, we have to stop and laugh, because if I am talking about Elijah, she looks at me and says, "Are you sure that's not my husband you are talking about?" Maybe they are twins, separated at birth.

After about two months of trying to get Marjorie to go out with him, Norman had to sit down and plan this out; he was determined to be married to her before the year was out. He had already wasted too much time; he had only nine months before she would become Mrs. Norman White. He was going to get her to notice him as being more than the man who picks up her garbage.

One morning, he had just gotten to her street when he saw her coming out of her house. He couldn't believe that he was so much in love with this woman and had never even been on a date with her; but that was about to change.

Marjorie was so busy trying to get to the bus stop that she didn't notice there was a man following her. The bus was coming and she didn't want to miss it. She saw that there were several people already waiting. Usually, she was aware of her surroundings, but that morning, she was rushing. That day would be the first time that she would spend all day in court as an assistant to one of the best lawyers in the state, maybe any state. She was so excited!

The bus was there; people were getting on. Just as she stepped on the bus, she felt a tug on her pocketbook—and it was off her shoulder and gone! She stepped back off the bus screaming, but the perpetrator was running down the street. He was looking backward, making sure that he was going to get away with what he had just done and ran smack into Norman so hard that it knocked him down. Norman reached down and picked up Marjorie's purse in one hand and was holding onto the perpetrator with the other. He yelled to his co-worker for help and to call the police. His co-worker rushed over and held the thief.

When Marjorie reached Norman, she was crying and thanking him, she was so happy to get her purse back. "Thank you, thank you! I am usually so careful. Thank you so much! Please, what can I do to show you how much I appreciate what you have done? Here, let me give you something for helping me get my purse back."

"Miss, I do not want a reward. I just happened to be here. I saw you rushing to get the bus and noticed you were being followed a little too close. I just did what any good citizen would have done. Now, if you will excuse me, I should get back to my work. I see the police are here, they can take over."

Marjorie spoke up, "Once again, thank you and...my name is Marjorie Johnson. What is your name?"

Norman didn't want to show his anxiety, but this was just what he wanted. "My name is Norman, Norman White." Marjorie thanked him one more time and went over to speak to the police officer.

Marjorie didn't know what had changed, but since Norman had gotten her bag back, she found herself looking for him on garbage day. It was a month before she saw him again and she was anxious to know where he had been. She couldn't believe that she was interested in the garbage man. She was at home with a cold and when she heard the truck outside, she hurried and got her coat and rushed out.

Norman was looking for her, also. He had purposely changed his route last month. He hoped he knew what he was doing, because time was of the essence, and he had to play this just right if this beautiful lady was going to be his wife this year.

They saw each other about the same time and she waited for him to stop and talk to her. He spoke to her. "Good morning, Miss Johnson." He picked up her garbage, told her to have a nice day and went on with his work. Marjorie was stunned. Here she was, sick with a high fever and had rushed out to talk to him and he acted like he didn't want to be bothered.

The following week the same thing happened; she waited until she saw the truck and then she proceeded to leave her house. This time, when she spoke to him, she started a conversation with him. "Hi, Norman, nice day; how are you?" He didn't want her to know that his heart was beating so fast. God, she was beautiful.

"Good morning, Miss Johnson. I hope you have a good day," and he kept on with his work.

Marjorie wasn't getting it. At first, he was interested; now, he didn't want to be bothered. Norman's plan was working. He could see that she was wondering what was going on. Now, he would go on to the next step.

In four months, they would be married. He was going to sweep her off her feet and once they were married, he was going to love her with all his being.

The following garbage pickup day, Marjorie didn't see Norman that morning. She walked slowly to the bus and let the first one go by; she was hoping to see him. Where was he?

Unbeknownst to her, Norman was waiting down the street; he had taken the day off. He had noticed that her lawn was a mess; he was going to work all day and surprise her when she came home. He was having a nursery make a delivery to Marjorie's house that morning at 9:30. He was happy to see her finally get on the bus and leave; he didn't want his plan to blow up in his face.

THE PERFECT RELATIONSHIP

Norman worked all day. The yard was beautiful. Some of the neighbors wanted to know if he was a gardener. They wanted him to do their yards.

When Marjorie came home, she had to look at the address to make sure she was at her house. Her yard hadn't looked that beautiful in a long time, not since her father was alive and did it. If her father and mother were alive, they would love to see how beautiful the yard looked now. Who did this? Marjorie saw her neighbor and was about to ask her if she had seen anybody in her yard that day, when she saw Norman walking towards her.

"Hi, I hope you like your yard. I thought that as beautiful as this house is, it deserves to have just as beautiful a yard."

Marjorie was stunned. "Norman, why would you go out of your way to do this? We hardly know each other, and don't you think you should have asked me first? I can't afford to pay you for this. Since my folks died, I can hardly afford to pay the taxes on this place, with school and all the other expenses."

Norman reached out and took Marjorie's hand. When she didn't object, he started to speak.

"Marjorie, I am sorry, I should have asked you. I love this house. When I was assigned to this route, the first time I saw this house, I thought it was the most beautiful house. When I saw that you lived here, it became even more beautiful. Please, I don't want you to pay me any thing for making this yard beautiful. I did it because I wanted to. I did it not to impress you, but because I saw it needed to be done.

"Marjorie, please don't think I am a crazed man, because I am not. I want you to know right now that I think you are the most beautiful woman I have ever seen. I know that you might think that I am out of my league, I mean me being a garbage collector and you becoming a lawyer. But I believe that if I have something to say, I am going to say it. We haven't gone out on a date and we may never. I feel you would be ashamed to go out with me, you might not want your friends to know what I do for a living; you might be wondering what I have to offer you. I feel that if you go out with me, get to know me, you might just like me. I know if you let me, I will shower upon you love that no other man could possibly give. The first time I saw you, I knew you were meant for me. I prayed and asked God to touch your heart, to lead you to me."

Marjorie was stunned. "You...prayed for me?"

"Yes Marjorie. I knew the first time I spoke to you that you are a kind person, that your heart is pure, good and loving. I asked God not to ever change your heart and to open your eyes to see me as someone with whom you could be happy. I promised Him that if He did, that I would love you and take care of you forever, that I would never ever do anything to hurt you."

Marjorie didn't know what to say, what to do. This man whom she had looked down on a few months back was now standing before her sending energy into her body with his mind. Damn, what was happening here?

Norman kept on talking. "Marjorie, if I could have but one wish, I would wish to wake up every day to the sound of your heart beating next to mine, the warmth of your body next to mine, knowing I could never find that feeling with anyone else. You bring a joy to my heart I have never known before. Of all the girls I have ever met, you're the one I could never forget. I know that God created you for me to love."

"Norman, please; what are you saying? We don't even know each other." They were still standing outside on her porch and she thought her neighbor was listening. "Norman, I usually

THE PERFECT RELATIONSHIP

don't do this, I don't know anything about you, but would you like to come in for a while?" She hoped she wasn't making a mistake by inviting him inside.

Once inside, Norman was a perfect gentleman; he made her feel so secure. She asked him if he would like something to drink, coffee or tea, that she didn't drink liquor or beer. She was shocked when he said to her, "Marjorie, you have been in school all day; if you don't mind, I will make you a cup of coffee or tea. Just tell me where everything is."

She had to look at this man. "Why?" she asked, "Why would you want to do that for me? You worked all day in my yard, I am sure that was harder than my being in class."

"Marjorie, you need to be pampered, and if you let me, I will treat you like the queen you are. You are special. I knew that the moment I laid eyes on you. Please relax. I promise I won't take advantage of you. You are my dream come true. Come, why don't you sit and relax? I'll take care of everything."

She led him into the family room. He lit the fireplace, took off her shoes and massaged her feet. Once he was sure she was relaxed, he went into the kitchen and not only made her tea but a nice dinner also.

Marjorie couldn't believe what was happening. Was this man for real? He was the nicest man, beside her father, that she had ever known. He was incredible. Was she falling for this man? She had dated a lawyer, a doctor, a pharmacist, a principal, but none could compare to this man whom she had not gone on one date with.

After they had eaten, they sat and talked. Before Norman left, he had asked her if she would go out with him that weekend, she had told him yes. In fact, she couldn't wait to be with him again.

Norman called on Thursday evening to confirm their date for Friday. He told her that he had a surprise for her. She couldn't wait to see him. She felt like a queen with this man; he was so easy to talk to. She couldn't believe that he listened to her. This man was unique. She found herself talking out loud. "God, is this the man of my dreams? The man my mother used to tell me that I would know was the one when I met him? Mom, I think he is the one; I have never been treated like this." She promised herself that she wouldn't rush into anything, that maybe this man was trying to get her into bed. She would be careful.

Friday night, Norman was on time. As she opened the door, she was amazed at how well he dressed up. He was a good-looking man. He helped her with her coat and they went out to the car. He opened the door for her and went around to the driver's side and got in. Before he started the car, he asked her if she liked it.

Marjorie was looking at him and was thinking, "Here we go. What is it with men and their cars?"

Norman started to smile. "Marjorie, remember the other night during dinner when we were talking about the yard, how happy you were to see it looking so beautiful again and how you wished you had the money to really fix up the house like it used to be? Remember you told me about your father's car that he had bought about three years before he died? You said that the car was in the garage and that you wish you could get it fixed but that you couldn't afford it. Marjorie, I hope you won't get upset with me; this is your father's car. I have a brother who is a mechanic. I had him to come and look at it. It's in good condition. It's ten years old, but it's a Mercedes; they are usually good cars. I had him to paint it and do whatever had to be done. He said that if you don't want it, he will buy it. I told him you were going to keep it.

THE PERFECT RELATIONSHIP

"Now you won't have to worry about getting the bus anymore, or going to the market and getting a taxi back home with your groceries. Since it's been sitting for so long, the only thing left is for me to drive it tonight a little distance to make sure its safe for you to drive. I want you safe."

She hadn't even missed the car, probably because she hardly ever went into the garage.

"This is one of my surprises—and the other surprise is that since tonight is Friday night and you don't have school tomorrow…I am taking you to Virginia Beach. Tomorrow, we are going sightseeing and we will come back early Sunday morning, if it is alright with you."

Marjorie was looking at him, and couldn't find the words to say anything. She was a little afraid; she had never spent the night with a man before.

Norman saw the way she was looking and knew she was afraid that maybe he was going to take advantage of her. He had to reassure her that he would never harm her. He took hold of her hand. "Marjorie, trust me, I will not hurt you."

She relaxed; she knew if he said he wouldn't hurt her, he wouldn't.

The drive to Virginia Beach was nice; Norman was a good driver. Once they got to the hotel, she again became nervous. Norman could sense that she was a little tense. When they got to the check-in desk, Marjorie was about to tell him she wanted her own room. She was not going to sleep in the same room with him. But before she could tell him he told the clerk who he was and that he had reservations. The clerk told him that his reservation was for adjoining rooms, they were ready and the things he had ordered had been put into the rooms. She gave him their keys.

Norman took hold of Marjorie's hand, put it to his lips and kissed it. "Baby, please relax. I am going to take care of you."

"Norman, I do trust you, but it just dawned on me that I didn't pack any clothes; I only have what I am wearing. I can't wear these clothes all weekend! I was so excited about the car; I didn't even think to go back into the house to pack something."

Norman was now opening the door to Marjorie's room. He led her in. Marjorie took one look and burst out crying. It was beautiful. There were red roses everywhere. Norman guided her to the closet and opened it. "You are a size eight, aren't you?"

Inside the closet were the most beautiful clothes, and on the bed, were the sexiest nightgowns.

Norman told Marjorie that he was going into his room to get ready for dinner and that when she was ready she could knock on his door. "And Marjorie, please wear that little black dress. I think you will look fantastic in it."

She couldn't believe what was happening to her. She hadn't known this man very long and he knew so much about her. She had never dated a man that would take the time to do what Norman had done—and how did he know she was a size eight?

"This man is a keeper," she thought. The men she had dated rated a zero next to him.

In his room, Norman couldn't keep his mind off Marjorie. He was in love with her. She was already deep inside of him. It was like that song that Percy Sledge sang; when a man loves a woman, can't keep his mind on nothing else, he'll trade the world for the good thing he's found.

This woman, he felt, was created just for him. "I don't know what it was that drew me to her," he thought out loud. "I have dated beautiful women before, but this one, I loved her the minute I saw her. And the sight of her set my pulse to race. I have not even kissed her and yet I love her so. She's perfect."

He had just finished getting dressed and was waiting for Marjorie; he was getting ready to go knock on the door when he heard her soft knock. Even though he had just left her, he couldn't wait to see her.

When he opened the door, she took his breath away. The dress was a perfect fit. Before he could say anything, she walked over to him, put her arms around him and kissed him. He held her close. As badly as he wanted to continue to hold her, to feel her, he let her go and escorted her downstairs for dinner.

As they walked to the dining room, Marjorie felt like the luckiest woman in the world. All eyes were on them. The women couldn't seem to keep their eyes off Norman, nor the men off her.

Marjorie was thinking to herself. "I said it already, and I have to say it again, he sure dresses up well. I can't believe that this man wants to be with me. And a few weeks back I was ready to turn my back on him because of what he does for a living. God, please forgive me. This man, I am never going to let go."

After dinner, Norman and Marjorie walked down to the beach; it was such a beautiful night. They found a cozy spot on the boardwalk and sat and talked for a while.

Marjorie found that they had so much in common; he was so easy to talk to. It was hard to believe that they had come from completely opposite backgrounds and, yet, they were so compatible.

He told her that he had gone to Hampton University for two years, but due to financial constraints, he had to drop out. He told her that she wouldn't be seeing him on the garbage truck anymore, because he had taken the test for inspector for the sanitation department and had passed. He would be starting his new position next week. He wanted her to know everything there was to know about him. Most of all, he wanted her to know that he loved her and wanted to marry her. That if she let him, she would have a love that she would never have to doubt.

"Marjorie," Norman spoke out. "If you will let me love you, I promise to give you all I have to give. Because of you, my world is now whole. When you need love, my heart I will share. You are my completeness, my eternal peace of mind."

"Norman, I think I am falling in love with you, also. But I don't want to think it; I want to know it. Please give me a little more time. You make me feel so special. I want to make sure that I am in love with you and not all the things you are doing for me."

He reached out and took Marjorie's hand. "Marjorie, our life together right now is already amazing; and you and me together, it can only get better. I will forever be grateful that you came into my life and made all my dreams come true. Together, we're perfect and I will enjoy spending the rest of my life with you."

Marjorie didn't know what to say, so she leaned over and kissed him on the lips. "I think we should go in now. We have so much planned for tomorrow. I want to go for a little swim before I go to bed. Let's hurry before they close the pool for the night."

Back at the hotel, they each went into their room to change into their swimwear. Marjorie knocked on Norman's door to let him know she was ready. As he opened the door once again, she took his breath away. She had put her hair back in a pony tail and had washed her face free of all make up. She was wrapped in a large bath towel.

When they were at the poolside, Marjorie was also amazed at how good Norman looked in a bathing suit. He was one fine-looking man. What a physique! He didn't wait for Marjorie; he dived into the pool and swam from one side to the other. When he got back to where she was, he came out of the pool. She was still standing there with the towel wrapped around her.

"Hey, lady, what's wrong? Can you swim?"

"Hey, mister, of course I can swim, my father taught me when I was just a little girl. But that water looks cold." By then, he was standing beside her. Before she knew what was happening, he picked her up and threw her into the pool, towel and all, and jumped in behind her. They were like children in the water.

It was getting late; the attendant told them that it was time to close the pool. Marjorie was the first to come out. Norman took one good look at her in the little blue bikini he had bought her, which he had just now gotten to see in full. Her body was beautiful.

Marjorie yelled at him, "Come, Norman! It's getting cold now and my towel is wet. We have to go." He came out of the pool.

Marjorie thought something was wrong with Norman; she went over to him. "Norman, what's wrong? You look so sad."

He looked up at her with tears in his eyes. "No, baby, I am fine. It's just that you are so beautiful." He took her hand. "I love you, Marjorie."

When they were in their rooms, each was thinking about the other. Norman wanted to go to Marjorie and make love to her. But he loved her too much to do that. He wanted her to feel safe with him and he didn't want her to think that was his plan all along, because it wasn't.

He had just fallen asleep when he heard a knock on his door and Marjorie calling out to him. He opened the door, and there she stood, looking like an angel. Once again, he was taken by her. He had to do all he could to keep from grabbing her. Instead, he asked her what was wrong.

"I am sorry to bother you, but I am not comfortable sleeping in hotel rooms. Usually, I put a chair back under the doorknob, but the chair in my room is too big to do that. Please can I sleep in here with you? I can sleep on the chaise lounge; it's large enough for me."

"Marjorie, you can sleep in the bed; I'll take the lounge."

"Norman, I trust you. We both can sleep in the bed. I feel safe with you and I know you won't make me do anything I don't want to do."

She went over and got into the bed; he followed. As he turned his back to her, she spoke to him. "Norman, can we talk for a minute?" He turned over, pulled her into his arms and they talked for about an hour before she fell asleep. He couldn't believe he had the most beautiful woman in the world right there in his bed and all they did was talk and hold each other tight. He wanted her to feel safe with him, and now she would. He respected her and would never hurt her, and now she knew that. "Thank you, God, for this woman who, in about three months, will be my wife."

The next morning, Norman awakened first. Marjorie had her head lying on his chest with her face turned towards his. She was gorgeous even while she was sleeping. He didn't want to wake her, so he watched her sleep.

When she opened her eyes, Norman was staring at her. "Good morning, have you been awake long? Why didn't you wake me?" she asked.

"Marjorie, to wake up and find you beside me is worth more than gold. You look so helpless when you sleep, like a child. You know you need me to take care of you. And you know that I am the only man that can do it."

147 | P a g e

Marjorie was beginning to really think that this man was THE ONE. If he were any of the other men she had dated, this would have never happened. They would have never just let her lay in bed and sleep. "This man is wonderful. He really respects me," she thought.

The rest of the weekend was glorious. They enjoyed each other's company so much. Norman was fun to be with. With everything they did, he made sure that it was what she wanted to do. As long as she was happy, he was also.

On Sunday, when they got back to Marjorie's house, she didn't want him to go. Norman told her that he felt the same way and, if it were alright with her, he would see her the next night, that he had another surprise for her.

"Another surprise? Norman, I don't know if I can take any more of your surprises. You are spoiling me!"

"Baby, you haven't seen anything yet."

She put her arms around his neck and kissed him. This time, the kiss was different, it lasted longer and he started to nibble on her lips, so gently. It was getting to her; she didn't want to let him go. He pulled away from her.

"Marjorie, I have to go. I don't want to, but I want to save everything we have for each other for our wedding night. I've told you, you are going to be my wife; I love you, woman." He turned to walk away.

Marjorie called after him. "Norman, wait, how are you going to get home? You don't have your car. I'll drive you."

"Marjorie, we have had a long weekend, you have school tomorrow. I'll take the bus. I'll see you tomorrow night."

She went into her house and closed the door. She was left alone with her thoughts. "Why wouldn't he let me drive him home? I was just beginning to feel comfortable with him. Is he holding something back? It was as if he didn't want me to see where he lives."

On the bus, Norman was hoping that Marjorie wasn't thinking about why he wouldn't let her drive him home. Tonight, he didn't want her to see where he lived, but if everything went according to his plans, tomorrow night she would see and know everything.

All day Monday, Marjorie was thinking about Norman. She knew that she was in love with him, what woman wouldn't be? She knew he loved her, also. But she was still a little skeptical; something wasn't right, especially when he wouldn't let her drive him home last night. What was he hiding?

Marjorie loved the car; it drove beautifully and it sure saved her a lot of time. She wouldn't have to leave the house so early in the mornings now and worry about taking two buses. She could now get to school in twenty-five minutes, and her part-time job was ten minutes from school instead of twenty.

When she returned home, there was a message from Norman. He would be there to pick her up at 6 p.m. He hadn't told her he was taking her anywhere. She thought they were going to have dinner at her house; she had even stopped and picked up something for dinner. What was he going to surprise her with now? He didn't tell her to dress up, so she put on some jeans.

Norman was on time, as usual. He seemed a little nervous.

"Wow, you even look beautiful in jeans. Ready?"

"Norman, wait, where are we going?"

"Please, baby, just trust me. You are going to like it. I promise."

He took Marjorie by the hand and walked her to the car. She had her hand on the handle when he stopped her. "Marjorie, when you are with me, I will open the door for you. You are my lady. Didn't I tell you that you deserve to be treated like a queen? To me that is what you are, relax."

Marjorie lives in Chesapeake. When she saw that Norman was getting on the expressway going towards Suffolk, she wanted to know where they were going.

"I am taking you to see your new house."

"What are you talking about? I have a house, a nice house."

"Yes, you do, and I like it, but the one we are going to live in after we are married, you will like more."

"Norman, married? We just met."

"Marjorie, please trust me. We should be there in another ten minutes." She decided to relax and wait and see what he was going to show her.

They got off the expressway and headed towards a community called Harbor View. It was a beautiful neighborhood. The houses there were gorgeous; all of them were different, unique in their own way. He turned into the driveway of a large house; it looked like a mansion.

Norman got out of the car, ran around to her side of the car and opened the door. He took her by the hand and led her to the front door, where he took out a key and opened the door into the most beautiful entrance hall Marjorie had ever seen. "Norman, whose house is this?" she asked.

"I want to show you something and then I will answer all of your questions." He guided her into a large living room and told her to take a seat, that he would be right back. He saw how nervous she was; he reached out and took her hand. "Everything is fine, baby, this is my house. Please stay calm. I will be right back. Trust me."

When he was gone, Marjorie had a chance to look around the room. This was some house, but she wondered how Norman could even afford this house.

Norman was back and he had a bottle of wine and two wine glasses. He sat everything on the coffee table and looked at Marjorie with so much love in his eyes. He reached in his pocket and took out a small jewelry box. He got down on his knees and took her hand.

"Marjorie, you are the most amazing thing that has ever happened to me. Each moment that you and I spend together is so magical that I catch myself smiling for no reason at all. I thought that I would never find someone like you. But now that we've found each other, I know that you are the person I want to spend the rest of my life with, the person I want to marry, the person I want to have babies with and the person I want to grow old with. Baby, you complete me. You make my life so wonderful and I don't know how else to repay you but to love you for the rest of my life. My world is a better place to be because of you. Marjorie, will you marry me?"

Marjorie couldn't believe what she was hearing. He had been telling her that he loved her and wanted to marry her, but they hadn't even known each other a year yet. He was moving too fast. There were some things she needed to know about, like this house, for instance.

Norman was waiting for her to answer. "Baby, I want to marry you. I know you love me. I told you that I will never hurt you and I promise to always protect you. What is it?"

"Yes, Norman, I love you, I love you so much. You make me feel so beautiful. You have shown me more love than I ever thought possible. But you scare me."

He took the ring out of the box and put it on her finger. "Baby, I am going to tell you right now everything you want to know. First, this house is mine. I bought it the first day I saw you. I had seen a for sale sign in the yard a couple of months before I knew you. The first day I saw you, I knew that I wanted you for my wife, and when I got off work I hurried over here to see if the sign was still in the yard, because I wanted it to be our house.

"I have lived in my brother's basement for fifteen years. Since I am handy around the house, he and his wife won't let me pay them any rent, because of my renovating their house for them. And believe it or not, the sanitation department pays me a good salary and most of it goes into the bank. I was able to put a good down payment on this house. Please, come let me show you your new house."

He gave her a tour of the house; first, the new kitchen he had put in all by himself. It had a large island that she loved, beautiful granite counter tops and the cabinets were beautiful—and so many. The pantry was larger than her bathroom at home. A large, open family room off the kitchen, with a built-in flat screen TV over the fireplace, was beautiful; and a living room just as large, with a fireplace.

The new his-and-her bathrooms that were in the master bedroom were fabulous and the large his-and-her walk-in closets were great. There was a balcony outside of the master bedroom it spanned from one side of the house to the other. The house had four other bedrooms, each with its own bath. There was a large theatre room with a wall-to-wall screen. There was an elevator that they took back down stairs. Outside, he showed her the yard. It had an in-ground pool. There was a large patio with an outdoor kitchen that looked better than what she had inside her house. The outdoor furniture was just as nice as what was in the house. It had a nice pool house, or guesthouse, also decorated nicely.

He took her back inside. "I did all the work myself with you in mind. What do you think? I love you and I would marry you tomorrow."

"Norman, I do love you. I was scared to love you at first, out of fear that you would hurt me, but I did and it's the best thing I've ever done. Now, the only fear I have is waking up and realizing it's all a dream. Thank you for giving me so much more than I ever could have wanted. I am so thankful for what we have and for everything we will have. You are the only man I ever want to share my life with. I could never imagine what it would be like if we were to lose each other. I don't even want to think about it. All I want to think of is you.

"Yes, I will marry you and, Norman, we can get married as soon as possible. I want nothing more than to be your wife.

"I love this house, but what about my house? My parents left it to me and I feel saddened knowing that I am going to leave it. And it needs a little fixing up."

Norman assured her that he would do whatever had to be done. He told her he knew a realtor and he would call him, if it was alright with her.

The realtor called Briana and an appointment was made to see the house. Briana asked all her friends to come with her. We couldn't wait to see this house that the realtor had told us would be perfect for Briana, and it was. We all liked it and we liked Marjorie also. Marjorie liked us; she didn't have any close friends, being in law school, and work kept her busy. She even invited us to her wedding.

For the next few weeks, Norman and Marjorie and her newfound friends were busy planning the wedding. Marjorie so wished her parents were alive to see her marry the man of her dreams. She would have loved for her father to walk her down the aisle and for her mother to have helped her pick out her dress. She couldn't believe how happy she was and how lucky she was to have a wonderful man like Norman to love her. And what was so amazing was that she had known him for only eleven months. Wow, she knew no one who had fallen in love so quickly and married so fast. All she knew was that she loved Norman and that he loved her.

The wedding was beautiful. Norman and Marjorie decided to incorporate vows they had written for each other into the traditional vows:

"I, Marjorie, take thee, Norman, to be my husband and before God and these witnesses, I promise to be a faithful and true wife. Since day one, we've shared something incredible, something that most people only dream of. You have made me the happiest I have ever been. You are a sincere, caring, loving man and I wouldn't trade you for the world. I am so thankful and blessed that you love me as much as I love you and that you want me for your wife. You make me feel like no one else could; you love me so sincerely and you are food for my soul. You are the love of my life. I love you, and I always will until the day I die. Hopefully, when that day comes, I will still have you by my side and yours will be the last face that I see."

Norman was so overwhelmed by Marjorie's vows; he had tears in his eyes.

"I, Norman, take thee, Marjorie, to be my wife and before God and these witnesses I promise to be a faithful and true husband. Marjorie, I didn't have to think twice when I asked you to be my wife. I knew that you were the perfect match for me. I don't think that there is, or that there ever could be, anyone better than you out there for me. I love you. I love every little thing about you. I love your cute smile, your magical eyes and the sound of your voice. I love your gentle touch and I love the warmth I feel when I'm by your side. I can't stop thinking about you when we are apart. You mean the world to me. You are the one I've always wished for. I never thought that I would ever meet someone as special as you."

Pastor Whitehead spoke up. "That was beautiful; now if you two are finished, I can go on with the ceremony."

"Will you, Marjorie, have Norman to be your husband? Will you love him, comfort and keep him, and forsaking all others, remain true to him as long as you both shall live?"

Marjorie almost yelled her answer, "I WILL."

"Norman, will you put the ring on Marjorie's finger?"

Marjorie continued to repeat after Pastor Whitehead. "With this ring, I do wed, and all my worldly goods, I thee endow. In sickness and in health, in poverty or wealth, till death do us part."

After Norman had repeated the same and said, "I most certainly will," Pastor Whitehead pronounced them man and wife.

Marjorie and Norman honeymooned in Hawaii. Norman had told her that she could go anywhere she wanted. She had always wanted to go to Hawaii or Paris. She couldn't choose which one, so Norman told her that he would flip a coin and that would be the place they would go, and for their first anniversary, they would go to the other place.

What a man, what a man!

———————————

Marjorie still couldn't believe that she was now married to this wonderful man, who she knew really loved her. She quivered to think that she had been looking down on him because he was a garbage collector and if he hadn't been persistent, she would have lost him. Marjorie prayed, "Thank you, God, for his persistence. I am the luckiest woman in the world. We have been married now for one year. And I cherish every moment since the day we met. I love him more and more every day. Thinking about our future fills me with anticipation and excitement. We make the perfect husband and wife team.

"We just found out that I am going to have a baby; if it's a boy we will name him Norman, Jr. If it's a girl, her name will be Taylor. I cannot wait for this baby to arrive. We are going to have a wonderful life together raising our family. All my dreams are coming true. I just love our new home and, God, I want to thank You so much for making it possible for us to live in such a beautiful place."

Norman was also excited about his life with Marjorie. She was everything he ever wanted in a partner and more. He had never been happier. She told him that it was God who had brought them together; that when he had told her that he had prayed for her, she had gone herself to God in prayer; she wanted to know if he was the one. They, as a couple, had started to pray together.

Norman prayed, "Heavenly Father, I know that we can make it through and get to that place where we'll have all we ever wanted. Look how much we have already! We have so much to be thankful for. We will just continue to lean on each other, loving and supporting one another with all the love we have. We will continue to put You in the midst of all we do, and as long as we continue to do that, we will be just fine."

Marjorie prayed, "Lord, thank You for not letting me walk away from this man. We women go through our lives trying to find someone that we think we would prefer to be our husbands. If he does not have a college degree, we don't want him; if he doesn't have a specific salary, we don't want him; if he's not good-looking enough, doesn't dress to please us, we don't want him. Lord, I want women to know that they are missing out on love because they are out there looking for the wrong things. I want them to know that they need to stop looking and start feeling the man that has found them, the man who has searched them out. Just maybe, he is the one.

"I am a lawyer, married to a garbage collector. I prefer him to any lawyer I know, any man I know. He may be a garbage collector on his job, but at home, he's my king who treats me like a queen. Lord, I just want to thank you for my husband, the man of my dreams."

Norman, Jr. was born twenty months after they were married, and two years later, they had their daughter, Taylor. They are the perfect couple with the perfect family. As Marjorie was tucking her children in one night, she had tears in her eyes. She looked at them as they slept and softly recited a verse from her favorite poem:

"I thank you my love for being there,
When I needed you the most?
Your caring heart has made me whole.
Your caring ways took over my soul.
You are my perfect love!"

THE PERFECT RELATIONSHIP

What is there to comment about in this relationship, except it is exceptional? They were perfect for each other. There was trust and respect. Marjorie trusted Norman and he had the utmost respect for her. He showed her that he was trustworthy and she showed him that he could be trusted. He did and said all the right things. He was an overall fantastic guy. His strengths complimented her weakness.

Genuine, enduring relationships are built on trust. With trust, intimacy can grow. They completed each other.

Your joy and satisfaction should be based on your ability, not someone else loving you. You need to know what makes you happy and not be dependent on someone else doing it for you.

Are there really men out there like Norman? Of course, there are. Hopefully, you all out there that haven't found him yet, will.

Norman and Marjorie, two imperfect people, creating the perfect relationship.

Chapter 6

Briana

Briana is the youngest of the group and is not married. She is an actress and travels all over the country. Her permanent home is in Chesapeake, Virginia; she bought Marjorie's house. She loved it the moment she saw it—and when she found out that Norman was quite handy and had done some of the renovations himself, she had him to renovate the whole house, adding two more bedrooms with baths and an in-ground pool.

Briana is quite pretty and reminds me of a younger Lena Horne. She has dated several men; two of them she thought would make good husbands, yet she is still single. She says she is a woman who knows what she wants in a man and is not going to settle for anything less. Yet, a man comes along who has all the qualifications she wants, and she won't marry him

So, I asked Brianna what she was looking for in a man this is what she said.

"I will start off by saying it's hard for a woman to find a good man these days. There are men out there that I can date, even marry, but I don't want just any man—I want a man that will be compatible, understanding, confident, has a good sense of humor and is a gentleman. He must not be selfish and should be able to compromise, not just with me, but also my family and friends. He should be able to talk to me when I am upset with him and won't right away think that it's that time of the month. But most of all, he must love me with all his heart. When he looks at me, he should become weak in his knees and compare all women he meets to me. If he wants me to be his wife, then he must be able to take care of me and provide for the family we will have. He must be financially stable.

"I am twenty-nine years old and have a wonderful career; I have a beautiful home that I bought myself and three very nice cars. I can buy my own clothes and I have more money in the bank than any man I have ever dated. I don't need a man to buy me material things. I know what type of man I want and need and I am not going to lower my standards to just have a man.

"I am not saying that he must make or have as much money as I do. But I am not going to settle for a man with poor financial standing, who is financially irresponsible and has other women besides me. Some men would look at this and say, 'Who does she think she is?'

"My grandmother once told me that a man wants a lady who is classy, intelligent, can hold her own in conversation with the best of them, who looks good on his arm—a trophy—and is a whore in his bed. I am all that.

"My self-esteem is very high; I know who I am and what I want. I am not phony. What you see is what you get. I am happy in my skin and I don't have to think like a man and act like a woman to get a man.

"To me, men are just like women. Figuring out what they want is not easy. Men come in all variations just like us and they have standards that they look for in women, just like we do in men. As I have already mentioned, my self-esteem is high. So, if I am all that and I know I am, what is wrong with trying to find my prince charming, why would I settle? Settling to me means that you don't think you can find the man that had the qualities you want, so you take whatever you can get.

DR. CAROLYN WHITE-BROWN

"I want to be desired, chased and admired by men. I want to be appreciated. Men say that I want too much, that I have to lower my standards to find a man. They tell me that I am conceited. Why, because I know what I want? I know I deserve the best. I love me. I am the one who has to create for me the life I want. If I have to wait for the person I feel is right for me, then I will wait.

"My father always told me that when it comes to men, I should never lower my standards in what I want; if a man is really interested in me, he will come up to mine. Men say they don't understand me. Well, they aren't easy to understand either. You give them your all and they lie and cheat and when you think you have finally met the man that could be the one, he turns out to be nobody you would want to spend the rest of your life with.

"Now this leads me to tell you about Tommy. Tommy was an actor in one of my movies. We were filming in Paris. One day, he asked me out. I was a little skeptical at first. I wasn't looking to date at that time, my career was just getting started and I was focused on that. It was my first big movie and the pay I received was more than I had made in the last two years put together. Tommy knew I had money and set out to get as much of it as he possibly could. All he saw was the money. I wanted someone who would see plain old, country girl, me—a nice girl, intelligent. The 'within me,' instead of the 'movie star' me.

"The first time I went out with him, I knew he wasn't my type, but I was so far away from home and lonely (mistake number one). I didn't know anybody. I worked with him, so I thought it would be alright; I mean after all, he was a very handsome man. He had been living in Paris for four years and knew how to get around. I wasn't looking for any relationship with him, just someone to have fun with.

THE PERFECT RELATIONSHIP

"It started out bad, right from the beginning. The first place we went, he claimed to have left his wallet back in his apartment. Next time, he claimed he hadn't had the time to go to the bank, asked me to please pay and said he would give it back to me the next day. At first, I thought he was sincere, that he really had left his wallet. I kept on going out with him; I was lowering my standards. I didn't even like him. As I said, I just wanted someone to hang out with. This man was taking me out to carry-out places and dumb movies that only he enjoyed. He was having a good time at my expense. He was a leech, the kind of man that thinks he's God's gift to women and will use them any way he can.

"He even had the nerve to think I would go to bed with him; that I was in love with him, but was playing hard to get. You may know the type. He tells you he loves you and you are the only woman for him, and you find out that he had told that to every other woman. Why do men think we are fool enough to believe everything they say? I told him that I wasn't interested in him and he really thought I was. Maybe he felt that way because I kept on going out with him (mistake number two). It was better than staying in my apartment when I wasn't working and it gave me the opportunity to see Paris. But really, after a while you ask yourself" Why bother"? I had to get rid of this idiot.

"I made reservations to go to the opera and, later, a very nice and expensive restaurant. The opera was excellent and I paid, because I had really wanted to go. The food was fantastic at the restaurant. I made sure that I ordered the most expensive items on the menu. And a one-thousand-dollar bottle of wine.

"After I finished my dessert, Tommy motioned for the waiter to bring the check. Just as I thought, he asked me if I would use my credit card, because he had left his at home. I stood up, told him that dinner was on him and walked out with him calling for me to please come back.

"The next day was my last day on the set. The movie was finished. Tommy didn't show up. I found out later that he was in jail. I didn't ask why, I knew why. I found out also that he owed a few people money. He spent his money as fast as he received it. He was broke.

"My parents raised me to know I should always go out with a man who would be able to take care of me. Tommy was only a co-worker; I was lonely and needed a friend to hang out with while so far from home. I had made a big mistake by going out with him in the first place. He was a user.

"I knew it was my fault what had happened. I was lonely; a lot of us go out with the wrong guy because of loneliness. That taught me that from then on, I would deal with someone on my level. Even though I wasn't looking for anything from Tommy, I lowered my standards; I would not do it again.

"Six months later, I was in California doing another film and met the man of my dreams; at least I thought he was. We were attracted to each other right away. His name was Michael.

"Michael, to me, was the ideal man. I had never met anyone like him. My thoughts of him were: he's kind, pleasant, reasonable and acceptable and he was livable. I knew that I could live with him, be comfortable with him. Yes, he was ideal. I fell madly in love with him. I had no warning signs about him. He was the one. I didn't have to tell him what I wanted in the relationship; he treated me beautifully, like a princess.

"Michael told me I could tell him whatever was on my mind, that he was not a mind reader and he loved it when a woman had the strength and was confident enough to tell him what she wanted. He told me that was the only way he could please me and give me what I needed. 'Wow!' I said, 'Your mother sure raised you right.' He told me that they were close. Later I would find out how close.

"I was head over heels in love with him. He was financially stable, confident and he could provide for a family. This man was wonderful to me. I didn't have to worry about how I looked all the time; you know when you are with your man you want to look nice, but not always dressed up. You want to be able to let your hair down, put on worn jeans, old blouses. I felt so secure in this relationship. When I didn't have on make up, he would say, 'Baby, you are beautiful even without your make up. You are the most beautiful woman I have ever seen.' When we were together, he never looked at other women. Once, I noticed a very beautiful woman in the coffee shop we were in. I pointed her out to him. He reached for my hand and said, 'Briana, she doesn't have anything on you. When I see a beautiful woman, I compare her to you.' Damn, he was good! I thought the way he treated me must have been how his mother raised him. Most women can appreciate a man who is close to his mother.

"Our relationship was good for a year. Everything was fine between us. He asked me to marry him and gave me a beautiful engagement ring. We were making plans to get married. He wanted me to meet his mother; things went downhill from there. I didn't have a clue of what was going on in his life concerning his mother.

"Michael was living in California; his mother in Florida. I didn't know it, but his mother was his manager and did everything for him. Controlled his money, handled all his businesses, had flown to California to decorate his apartment and bought most of his clothes. Ladies, this man whom I was so in love with was a mama's boy. And mama was about to tear down what I thought was solid between Michael and me.

"I had always thought of him as long term. I had tested the waters and I knew how he would react in most situations. That was before I found out that he was a mama's boy. As long as it was me and him, things were great, but when mama was around, everything started to fall apart.

"The day had finally arrived for me to meet his mother. We flew to Florida. Mama started to take over at the airport. We hadn't even gotten off the plane good, when she saw us. She ran right to Michael and started yelling, 'My baby's home, my baby's home!'

"Michael introduced me. She said, 'So this is my daughter–in–law to be; let me see that ring.' I put my hand out and she almost fainted. 'This ring is gorgeous! How much did you pay for it, Michael? You should have called me; I could have gotten it cheaper. You know I handle your affairs. Tomorrow, we'll go and exchange it for a cheaper one. You won't mind, will you Betty?' I was waiting for Michael to speak up; when he didn't, I did.

"'My name is Briana and yes, I do mind! This is the ring Michael gave me, he picked it out; I love it and I am going to keep it, isn't that right Michael?' He looked at me and said, 'Briana, my mother may be right. I did pay a lot for it. I should have called her to tell her I was buying the ring. We are going to be here for a few days. I went to Jared, and there is one here in Florida. You can pick it out yourself, just a cheaper one.'

"Well, I wanted to scream, but decided to save it for later when I really had to. What happened to: I could tell him whatever was on my mind, that he was not a mind reader and he loved it when a woman had the strength and was confident enough to tell him what she wanted, that was the only way he could please me and give me what I needed?

"My sweet, loving Michael, the man I was so in love with and wanted to marry was now acting like a little boy. He was totally dependent on his mother telling him what to do. I just couldn't believe what was happening. Mama was taking over and Michael was letting her. Once we got to the house and after we had dinner, she started planning the wedding.

"Betty" …" It's Briana, I spoke up."

"Well, whoever," she said. 'Tomorrow, I will show you the house I bought for Michael and you to live in. It's only three blocks from here. Michael, you will love it. Also, I have already told your cousins that they will be bridesmaids."

"'What??? Excuse me, Mrs. Knight, but I have my own bridesmaids.'

"It's okay, dear, they can be guests; I have already told Michael's cousins they would be his bridesmaids."

"I spoke up again, Mrs. Knight, I don't want to hurt your feelings, but it's Michael's and my wedding and I will choose who I want to be in it and as I said, my friends are going to be my bridesmaids."

Mama looked at Michael and asked him what he had to say. I was expecting this man to take my side, but he told her that he would talk to me about it later, that right now all he wanted to do was get some sleep.

"This woman had no regard for my feelings. I started to pray silently to calm down "God, I need You right now to intervene with what I am about to say and do to this woman. Please, God. I need Your help right now, because this woman is about to get an old-fashioned beat down and then I know I will have to take her son on after that."

"I couldn't believe what was going on; I had never been with Michael and his mother in the same place. He talked about her all the time. How she had raised him after his father died, how she always put him first. He told me once that he would always be there for her and the woman he married would have to understand that. I didn't have a problem with that. Sons who are close to their mothers seem to be more caring, more willing to express emotions, more respectful to women. I think this is the type of man most women would prefer. But there is a difference between being close to your mom and being a mama's boy. I was seeing a side of him I had never seen before.

"Michael was always considerate of how I felt. But around mama he was different. The next day, we went for our morning run. I thought this was a good time to bring up what his mother had said the night before. Wrong idea! He reminded me that he was her only child and all she had, that she was really a nice person and he asked for me to please try and get along with her.

"'Okay,' I said, 'but I am keeping my ring and you have to tell her that you are not going to get a cheaper one.'

"At breakfast, I learned that Michael was never going to say no to his mother. By the time I came down, Michael and his mother had already decided on my ring. She was very nice to me and for once said my name right.

"'Good morning, Briana. I have a wonderful surprise for you. She went over to the counter and came back with a beautiful jewelry box. This ring belonged to my great grandmother. Michael and I would like for you to have it as your engagement ring. Isn't it beautiful?' I looked at Michael.

"'Please, Briana,' he said. 'Look at it; it is beautiful and it cost more than the one you are wearing.'

"I took the box and looked at it; it was beautiful and he was probably right about it being more expensive, but the one he gave me, I really liked.

"Mrs. Knight spoke up. 'Please try it on Briana; if it doesn't fit we can have it sized when we go to Jared to take the other one back.'

"I said, 'Michael, may I speak to you in private, please?'

"Mrs. Knight spoke up. 'It's okay Briana; I am going to get dressed. We have a lot to do today, and my nieces are meeting us downtown to pick out the bridesmaid dresses. And speaking of dresses, I want you to wear my wedding dress that I married Michael's father in. It may be a little big on you, but it can be altered. Didn't Michael tell you about it? I won't be long; I'll see you in about fifteen minutes."

"It was now time to scream.

"When she was gone, I looked at Michael and said, 'Please tell me what just happened here. The ring is beautiful, but it's not the one you got down on your knees and proposed to me with. I really like my ring, Michael, and I am not going to give it back. I am not going to wear your mother's wedding dress and my friends are going to be my bridesmaids.

"'Now, Michael, you have to tell your mother that we have discussed this and you and I are planning our wedding; she can help, but the decisions are ours.' The look he gave me, I knew it was over.

"Briana, she is my mother; she doesn't mean any harm. She has always taken care of my affairs. I won't hurt her feelings.'

"Your affairs? I thought our getting married included me. Your mother won't even let me pick out my own dress, our own house and bridesmaids. I am getting married and I don't know my bridesmaids. And Michael, you let her buy a house for us and you never mentioned it to me—and it's down the street from here! I have a house in Virginia and we both have condos in California.

How many residences do we need? Even if we did buy one here in Florida, it surely wouldn't be three blocks from your mother!

"'I am not asking you to stop being close to your mother. I want you to remember that I am the woman in your life. I am going to be your wife. You may need your mother telling you what to do, but I don't. You are thirty-four years old. Your mother needs to understand that she raised you as a child and now that you are an adult, you can make your own decisions. I know a lot of mothers find it hard to let go of their babies, but Michael, your mother is controlling you.'

"He spoke up. 'Briana, ever since we got here, you have picked on my mother. As I have said, I am not going to hurt her feelings, if she wants to help us save money, what's wrong with that?'

"Mama walked in. 'Well, are we ready, Michael? Do you have the receipt for the ring? Briana, let me see how my great grandmother's ring looks on your finger. You know, one day you and Michael might have a son, and when he gets married, you could give him the ring to give to his wife, that way it stays in the family. Come, let's go; I want you to meet your bridesmaids.'

"That did it. I had had enough. 'Mrs. Knight, I told you that my friends are going to be my bridesmaids. I am keeping my ring and I am not going to wear your wedding dress. Now if you and Michael want to go wherever it is you are going, go, but I am not going with you.'

"Michael came over to where I was standing. 'Briana, please, this is my mother. She is only trying to be helpful, please come with us. I promise, you can pick out your wedding dress and your friends can be your bridesmaids. I love you, you know that.'

You love me? No, Michael, you don't.'

THE PERFECT RELATIONSHIP

"Mrs. Knight had to put her two cents in. "Briana, stop acting like a child. My son says he loves you. That should be the only thing that matters. He could have had his pick of dozens of girls and he picked you. Now stop acting like a baby and come with us, I have so much to do today. I have to go to the church to see if the date we want is available."

"Mrs. Knight, didn't Michael tell you that we are getting married in Virginia? Everything is all set there.'

"Yes, dear, he told me, but after I explained to him that all his relatives are here, I live here and I want him to get married in the church me and his father got married in, he understands how important that is to me. It's a beautiful church; you will love it. I'll take you there before you two go back to California."

That was it. 'Michael, Mrs. Knight, please sit down and listen to what I have to say.

"Can it wait for later, dear? We really have to go,' his mother said."

Then why don't you go, Mrs. Knight; Michael and I will catch up with you later.

"Michael finally spoke up (about time). : Mom, please go on ahead, we will meet up with you later."

She had to say one last thing before she left.

"Well, come and give your mama a kiss, Peanut; and change your shirt, that's not the one I laid out for you to wear."

"Okay, mama, I'll change.'

"Thanks, Boo-boo,' she said. 'See you two later."

You see what I mean. Mama rules.

"After she had gone, I told Michael to please sit down and listen to what I had to say. 'Michael, I love you very much. I know you know that. But I can't marry you.'

"Briana, please, what are you saying? We were meant to be, I love you. Please don't say you won't marry me. It's my mother, isn't it? You don't like her.'

"I just met your mother. I must admit she is something, but it's not her, it's you. Michael, I really don't mind you being close to your mother, but close is not the word for it. The relationship you two have is strange. I wouldn't mind if you had a normal relationship with your mother, but clearly yours is abnormal. Just this morning, I had gotten up to go to the bathroom; you were in there Michael. I turned to wait until you came out, but I heard you talking to someone and when I peeped in, it was your mother in your private bathroom shaving your face. Remember when I wanted to shave you? You laughed and said no, because I might cut you. But mama can shave you.'

"Briana, my mother has been shaving me since the day I began; she taught me.'

"That's what I mean, Michael. I find that strange. Just because she taught you doesn't mean she has to continue to do so the rest of your life. You are a thirty-four-year-old man, Michael. Let go of her apron strings."

"You are just jealous, Briana!' he shouted.

"Jealous? Michael, I do like your mother, but I don't like what she is doing and when I speak up about it, you take her side. As I have stated, there is nothing wrong with you being close to your mother as long as you respect me and put me first. In the Bible, Genesis 2:24 says that when a man is married, he will leave his father and mother and be united to his wife, and they will become one flesh. I don't think you will ever do that, Michael. You will never leave your mother's side. If I marry you, you will always take your mother's side.'

"Briana,' he said softly, 'I will always be by your side. My mother is my mother. She will not be living with us. And I do come to your defense. Didn't I just tell my mother to go on, that we will catch up with her later."

"You call that coming to my defense? You go to hell, Michael! And no, you didn't come to my defense. You just told your mother to go on ahead. That wasn't telling her to let us plan our wedding ourselves. If I stay with you and let your mother have her say about our wedding, she will probably show up at the wedding wearing a tuxedo to stand beside you as your best man.'

"Please, baby, I am my mother's life, all she has. I don't want to cut her out of my life. She needs to feel needed.''

"What about me, Michael? I don't have a chance with you as long as your mother is around. Whatever she wants to do, when it comes to us, you let her. It's driving me crazy and making me sick. I know you are her only child; you don't have to keep reminding me of that. It's like she is competing with me for your love. She wants to make sure I know that she will always be first in your life. She is very bossy and doesn't mind telling us what to do.

"I am sorry, Michael, but I am not going to marry you and have your mother continue to boss us around. You obviously aren't going to cut the strings with her. So, I am cutting the strings with you. Here, give these rings to your mother.

"I am going upstairs to pack my bags; please call a cab to take me to the airport. I wish you and your mother the best and hope you and she find the perfect partner for you. Why don't you try a daddy's girl?'

"I was engaged to a mama's boy; luckily, I was able to break away before it was too late. Ladies, if you find out your man is a mama's boy, put on your sneakers and run."

DR. CAROLYN WHITE-BROWN

"Michael kept calling me for about three months straight, leaving messages saying he loved me and wanted me back. I thought about it until his mother called and asked me to please come back to her baby, that he was making himself sick over the breakup, that I had broken his heart. Can you imagine that, mama still doing things for him? I tightened my strings on my sneakers and ran faster!

"After that relationship, I put all I had into my work. I didn't date; I didn't want to. I knew that I would just wait on God and He would lead the right man to me."

"I was filming a movie in New York City, about a year after breaking my engagement to Michael, when I met Josiah. He was a cameraman on the set. I wasn't looking for any relationship. My mind was only on my career. I kept to myself. I found myself liking New York City so much that I bought a condo in Long Island. I had family there. It was nice to work in the City during the day and take the long drive back to Long Island at night.

"On Sunday, if I wasn't working, I would go to church with my cousin, King. King was a minister and he had the type of church that made you want to always come back. The sermons were always good, he could preach, the music was fantastic and one of the soloists could touch you with his singing—when he finished, everybody in the church was on fire with the Holy Spirit.

"One Sunday, after the service, the soloist came over to say hello. I didn't recognize him at first, and then it came to me where I knew him from. He was the cameraman on the set of the movie I was doing! I apologized to him for not recognizing him. From that moment on, we became friends. Josiah was so nice. I found myself liking him, but only as a friend. I was not ready to try another relationship. They all seem nice until you fall in love and commit yourself; next thing you know, it's not what you had thought it would be."

"For the next several months, we had good times together. I even invited him to come with me to my home in Virginia. I had a barbecue and told all my friends to come. They all liked him. Kayla told me later that her husband, Elijah, had really liked him and wanted to know if we were serious. Marjorie called me to say that he reminded her of Norman and wanted to know if we were a couple. Friends! Why can't they stay out of your business? The truth is, I was beginning to like Josiah. But I didn't want to get into another relationship and be sorry later.

"Driving back to New York, Josiah and I had a great time. We just took our time. Every time we saw a yard sale, we stopped. We found a nice restaurant in Delaware to have lunch and just before we got on the New Jersey Turnpike, we decided to go to Atlantic City. I was so relaxed with this man. Josiah drove most of the way. The last time a male friend drove one of my cars, he asked me if he could use it for one day and after two weeks, I had to call the police to get it back. I trusted Josiah; I found myself liking this man a lot. "

I am not going to say that he is the one for me. I said that about Michael and he wasn't. But I will say he could be. He has a lot of the qualities I want in a man. He's patient and very spiritual.

"Josiah has told me that he really loves me and wants to take the relationship a step further. I told him, 'Let's just take it one day at a time."

"He does have the qualities that I would like for my husband to have, but so did Michael. I did check what kind of relationship Josiah has with his mother. She's okay and he is not a mama's boy. He is honest and he respects me. He isn't afraid to talk about things and he seems to be interested in my life and what

I want. He is, so far, different than the type of man that I usually date. He would make a good husband. He is not the best-looking man I have dated, but he is the nicest.

"A week ago, he asked me out to dinner. He didn't tell me where we were going. It was the Four Seasons in New York City. Fine American cuisine is served there and you have to wait sometimes up to three weeks for weekend reservations. Everything was so beautiful. He had ordered a bottle of champagne; he said he wanted to celebrate. I wanted to know what he was celebrating and he took a jewelry box out of his pocket, got down on his knees right there in the restaurant and asked me to marry him."

"Everyone near us was watching. When he asked me the second time, I got up and ran out of the restaurant, crying hysterically. This man would be the ideal husband. I know he would be, but I can't marry him. I was so ashamed of running out on Josiah like that. For the next week, I did not return his calls. I had to get away for a while. It was time for our girlfriends monthly get together."

"I called Kayla to confirm I would be in Virginia by Wednesday and to remind her that the meeting was going to be at my house. I was looking forward to seeing everybody. I was going to fly, but it was only forty-five minutes by plane from New York to Virginia. I drove down on Monday; I needed time to think about what I was going to do concerning Josiah. I had hoped my friends wouldn't bring him up. Wrong! As soon as they were all in my house, they wanted to know why he didn't come with me. I explained to them that I had to distance myself from him for a while to think about our relationship."

"Briana, what is there to think about?' asked Marjorie. 'That man loves you. I can tell he adores you.'

"Yes, I know and he wants to marry me, but I can't marry him."

"Camille spoke out. 'Briana, you told us the last time you were here that he was the nicest man you have ever dated. What has happened that now you have changed your mind about him?"

"I haven't changed my mind about him. He is the nicest man I have ever dated and has all the qualities I want in a man. But haven't you all noticed? He is white."

"Kima got up, went over and sat by me. 'Sweetie, when I saw you and Josiah together, I said to myself, 'Here are two people who really love each other.' I wasn't thinking, 'Here are two people one Black and one White who love each other.' The way Josiah looks at you is like you are the only one in the room. His eyes are only focused on you. When Albert and I were at our best in our marriage, he never looked at me the way Josiah looks at you. So, he is white; tell me, if you could change his color would you marry him? If he was Black you would marry him? Here, look in this mirror, because I don't know if you have noticed, but girl, you look white."

"I got up and stood in the middle of the room and said, 'Look, all of you. Yes, I look white; some people have even thought I am white. But I am Black and both of my parents are Black. You all know my story. My mother's father, my grandfather—who won't acknowledge my mother—is white. I took after her side of the family. I am not concerned about Josiah's skin tone; I have the same skin tone. You all don't seem to understand what I am saying. He is white; his whole family is white. They like me now, but what happens when they meet my dark-skinned father and all my other dark-skinned relatives? What happens if we have a dark-skinned baby?

DR. CAROLYN WHITE-BROWN

"I have met Josiah's mother. I have to admit she is nice, but there is something about her that I can't put my hands on. The first time I met her, she asked me if I was Polish. I told her that I was Black. For a second, her facial expression changed. I don't want to have to keep going through that when I meet his family and friends. Right now, they think I am some famous, well-known movie star who makes a lot of money. You know, if you are Black and average, they (white people) don't want you anywhere near them. But Black and famous and rich, they don't mind. If you live next door to them, they love it. They run and tell their friends, 'Guess who lives next door to me?' But if you are just an average Black family just trying to make it in this world, they panic and move away. I have gone through that with my parents. I remember us being the first Black family moving into a neighborhood and within two years most of our white neighbors were gone.

"I don't want to have biracial children not knowing what race to belong to or pretending to be all white and being picked on by other children. When I was younger and kids would see my Black father and my white-looking mother, I was called a zebra by both Black and white kids. They were always pulling my hair and beating me up. I cut my hair very short and tried to have it look like an Afro. I thought if my hair was short, maybe my classmates would be my friends. I even found a makeup to make myself appear darker. I was always running, trying not to get beat up. I had one friend who was biracial. We understood each other. When we graduated high school, we even went to the same college to make sure we would have someone to talk to, a true friend. In college, things changed a little, the guys liked us but the girls were indifferent to us.

"I have always imagined what my husband would look like. He is tall, dark and Black. I want my husband to be completely, one hundred percent Black. Yes, I love Josiah and to answer your question, Kima, if he were Black, I would marry him.' "

"So, what are you saying?' Claudia added. 'This man is the nicest man you have dated and treats you like a queen. He's good enough to date, but not good enough to marry. Is that what you are saying? Because he's white you won't marry him?'

'Look, all of you, I will say this one more time. I have always dreamed of my husband as being tall, dark, handsome and Black, not tall, light and white. I cannot marry a white man.'

"Carol was listening to the conversation. Finally, she commented, 'Briana is he on the Down Low? Because if he isn't, I will take him.'

"Carol continued, 'I am not going to question you on this, but I want you to know that just the idea of thinking you have found your soul mate can really stress you out. You meet this wonderful person, finally, a man that just might be Mr. Right. He is everything you want in a husband. This is what most of us dream about. You think to yourself, is it true—that there is a man who doesn't make you want to get up and run every time he comes near you? Your heart beats fast when he calls your name and you get butterflies in your stomach when he comes near you, and when he kisses you, you know with all your heart that he is the one. And with all your heart you want to be Mrs. Right. This is what happened with Doug and me. I knew he was the one. And I knew also that he loved me. But he wasn't honest with me. He was a liar and a cheater and with a man.

"Briana, finding a man to love is easy. Finding a man that makes you happy, makes you feel good, is also easy. But the hard part is finding a man that can make you happy and makes you feel good without any of the insensitive side effects that some men always seem to create.

DR. CAROLYN WHITE-BROWN

"After Doug, I was reluctant to date. I didn't trust men. I didn't want to get hurt again. I did some soul searching. I always thought I knew me; I had to find myself all over again. I made sure I knew who I was, what my dreams are, what qualities I want my mate to have. Doug was a teacher for me. I haven't found Mr. Right yet, but I do know that there is a man for me—and when we find each other I don't care what color or race he is. As long as we love each other, are satisfied with each other, are friends—honest, open, respectful—and that doesn't change, then I am going to grab him, hold on tight and never let go. Briana, don't throw Josiah away waiting for your Black stallion to come galloping in—you may find yourself too old to ride him.' "

What would you do in Briana's situation? I am not even going to discuss Tommy; I am sure most of us have at one time or another come across a "God's gift to women" in our lives.

Michael is another story. To think that you have finally found your dream man, get engaged to be married, then you meet his mother and find out that two is company; three is a crowd. How distressing is that? It's hard enough finding your perfect man. Now you have to compete with mama, who time after time gets to have the final say. Some of us may try to stay in the relationship because we love him so and think we can stand up to mama. Please. I am no expert, but you'd better be ready to take on Mama Dearest.

Now, you finally have found someone who, to you, is the ideal man. He loves you, respects you, appreciates you—all the things you said you wanted in a man, he has. But because of his race, you won't marry him? Something to think about. Briana's story is not finished. Let's go on…

Chapter 7

Melody

Melody spoke up, "Briana, I am surprised at your thinking. Now we aren't telling you who to marry, but please don't let differences of race sabotage your relationship, your happiness. So, you are Black and he is white. You told us yourself when you brought him with you to meet us that he was so different from any man you had met, that he was exciting, fun, and that you loved each other. Isn't that what's important? You said he was someone you could go the distance with."

"Yes Melody, that is important, but I didn't think he wanted to marry me. Our relationship was perfect until he mentioned marriage. And I can't marry him. I won't marry him."

Melody got up and came over to Briana. "I am sixty-five years old. I am the oldest of this group. I have been married four times. I has failed three marriages before I realized who my soul mate was. If I hadn't been so bossy, so oblivious to the problems I was creating in my first marriage, I would have only had one husband and would have never gone through what I did with two men I simply hated being married to."

"Two men?" Briana asked. "I thought you said you have been married four times."

"Yes, I was. To my first husband, Robert, then Harold and Richard, and then I remarried Robert, who is still my husband now.

"Please listen to what I am going to say. You are Black and he is white, so what? You both are faithful to each other, that's a big connection right there. Forget race. I feel that is not the issue.

THE PERFECT RELATIONSHIP

What should really matter is how you as a couple actively deal with your emotional response to your differences. I always had in mind what my idea of a perfect marriage would be; and when I thought I had found the person to share it with, Robert, I set out to make sure it would last forever.

"Robert was the love of my life. I met him in college; we hit it off right from the beginning. After a few months of dating, we decided that we wouldn't see other people, that we liked each other very much. What a guy he was. We were young and in love. We would walk in the rain and loved it. When it snowed, we would play like kids in it, making snow angels. We were connected and involved in each other's lives. I felt secure with him. I knew that he would never leave me; that I would never be alone, I would always have him. He had the same moral values and social skills as I did. We were equivalent in intelligence. I truly loved him.

"We became engaged and had a beautiful wedding. The honeymoon was fantastic. Later, when we got back to our new apartment, things changed. We had always lived in separate apartments. I didn't know what it was like to live with anyone except my family. All I knew was that I loved my husband and wanted to make him happy. I found myself telling him what to do and where and when to do it. I was dominating the marriage. I took over everything. Instead of letting him have a say in things, I would say to him, 'I think we should do it this way.' I even told him to give his paycheck to me and I would take care of everything. I was clueless to what I was doing to him and when he left me, I couldn't understand why.

"He had told me he would never leave me. But that was before we lived together. When you are dating, everything is wonderful. You can't wait to see each other and when it's time to say goodbye, you hold on to each other for dear life. I didn't know the things I was doing were wrong. I thought I was being a good wife. When he didn't like the way things were going, he told me we had to talk. I wouldn't listen to him. I was trying so hard to please him, but I was really running him out of my life.

"I was always nagging him. You know I've heard that a nagging wife is like a dripping faucet, it drives you crazy until you fix it. That's what Robert did. He fixed it; he left me. Before he left, he told me that he was sorry but our marriage was a mistake. He said that he had an idea of what his wife would be like. That all men look for that one woman who has all the qualities that they are looking for in a woman. That each man will have his checklist of wishes, wants and needs and she would be able to fulfill every wish that he has. But if he finds her lacking, then he thinks to himself that she is not suitable or good for him; that he chose the wrong woman.

"Robert told me that he really thought that I was the one and even when I was dominating and wanting to take charge of the marriage, he still thought that we could work it out, that maybe he was asking for too much. But when I wouldn't listen to him, wouldn't give in, wouldn't let him get a word in and told him that my way was best, he knew then that he had married the wrong person. That another man might be happy with me and be quite content with my ways, but he wasn't.

"I asked him what he thought the perfect wife was. He told me that the perfect wife never nags, complains unreasonably or needlessly—even when there is reason to and would be right in doing so. She would never be unfaithful, even if her husband is unfaithful to her. She would confront him, talk it out and if they couldn't fix it, she would quietly divorce him. She would keep him happy in the bedroom. She's a good listener even if she doesn't want to be bothered with what her husband is saying. She doesn't do drugs, drinks casually and is a fantastic cook and housekeeper. She never talks underhanded about her husband to her friends—even if he deserves it—but tells them he is magnificent. She is always there to support him. She will help manage the money and, with her, he could save more than he anticipated they would. With her by his side, the moon is the limit. Men will look at her and want her, but he knows her heart will always be his. But of course, it works both ways."

"And then he said to me, "Melody, you know that no one is perfect. But just as women say they are looking for the perfect man, men are looking for the perfect woman." The truth is, when we find someone and we both commit ourselves, we then start to build our relationship and we then become perfect for each other."

"I thought you were that perfect someone for me, but you made yourself the wrong person. That is why I can't stay married to you. But just because you weren't the right wife for me doesn't make you a bad person. You are one of the nicest women I've ever met. May God bless you always and may you find happiness." And with that, he left me. Within six months, we were divorced.

"Next, I met Harold. He was good-looking and he knew it. He was absorbed by his looks. He was egotistical and selfish and had a history of cheating and abuse. I married him anyway, thinking I could change his ways. A lot of us women marry men thinking we can change them. Wrong. If you see what he is like before you marry him, why do you feel he will change after you marry him?

Harold had no respect for me. He would flirt with other women right in front of me. His women were always calling my house telling me that they were with my husband; that they had been in my house when I was out of town and had had sex in my bed; that Harold was going to leave me for them. One even came to my house saying she was in love with him and had the nerve to confront me telling me he wasn't happy with me and that she wanted to see what I looked like. Tell me, what would make a woman fall head over heels in love with another woman's husband? She told me that God told her that Harold was going to be her husband. That she had to come to tell me because God doesn't lie; that she was a Christian woman and she knew when God was talking to her. It's amazing what lies people tell on God!

"I stood there looking at this woman. My first instinct was to pull her into my house and beat her silly. Instead, I spoke to her.

"Honey, tell me, why would God send you over here to tell me that he has promised my husband, who is already married, to you? Are you so much in need of a man and men so few that you would want to settle for being someone that a married man cheated on his wife with? If I divorced him today and he married you tomorrow, what makes you think he would not cheat on you, if he cheats on me with you? What makes you think he'll be faithful to you? Why would you want to be someone a married man comes to just to have sex with? I don't know what my husband has told you, I really don't care, but he has problems, we have problems. If he's having trouble at home with me, he needs to come home and deal with it and not involve you in his drama. I want you to know that a woman who settles for a man who is married, in my opinion, has low self–esteem and a poor, negative image of herself. You should be able to dream higher than having somebody else's husband.'

There was so much I could have told this woman about Harold, but there was no need, she would later find out about him for herself. I never told Harold about this. Why? All he was going to do was lie about it. Harold was a piece of work. I tried so hard to fix what was wrong, but I couldn't do it by myself.

Once, his brothers and their wives came from Georgia to go to a family function; I knew about this because my sister-in-law had called and told me. I went shopping for something nice to wear. When the day arrived and his brothers and their wives came, we were all getting ready to go, when Harold looked at me all dressed up. "He yelled at me right in front of everybody, where in hell do you think you are going? You don't know anybody there and you are not going with me any damn place!" I asked him if he could please be nice to me for just one day; just pretend that he liked me for a change—just for an hour, a minute, a second.

"I felt like a fool. I knew Harold didn't love me and at that moment, I didn't love myself either. You know it's your birthright to wake up in the morning and feel loved, feel good about yourself. Loving you, looking at yourself in the mirror, liking what you see and telling yourself, 'Hey, look at me; I am a queen,' and feeling you got it going on.

"With Harold, it was like living with a rattlesnake. I had to be careful where I stepped at all times, because if I didn't, his tail would start to rattle and he would strike out at me.

"I didn't want to make a scene, so I calmly said, 'Excuse me, Harold. I went out and bought this beautiful dress and I had my hair done. I even had the car washed—and we are taking my car, right?' He said, 'What do you think?' I said, 'Oh, by the way, the car is mine and since you don't have one, you can find a way to get there.' Then I said to his brothers and their wives, 'Let's go, Harold is not riding with us.' We all went to the reunion and had a great time. We didn't even miss Harold. You see, he had planned on taking someone else.

"Now, Briana, I know you are wondering where this is leading. Please be patient and listen for just a few more minutes. Harold was a verbal abuser and controlling idiot. He would get jealous of me if he thought I looked better than him when we went out and once he even had the nerve to ask me to walk behind him. I told him, 'This is America, and I don't walk behind my husband,' and proceeded to walk beside him. I had made a terrible mistake with this man. There is no reason for a person to be talked down to and treated like they are nothing, especially when it's your mate.

"Did Harold love me? No, but still I stayed. I had made up my mind that I might as well stay with him, that there was probably no one else for me. I was pretending to myself, family and friends that I was perfectly happy with things, when really, I wasn't. I had settled for a man not worthy of my worth. I was a fool. Now, you tell me why any woman would want to stay with a man who abuses her. Are we getting so desperate that we will settle for anything just for the sake of having a man?

"I wasn't happy at home so I decided that I would do something to make me feel better about myself. I went back to school for my Master's. Well, all hell broke loose. Harold told me that I thought I was better than he was and when I would be studying, he would come over and knock my books off the table. He started to hide my car keys to keep me from going to school. I would have to call a cab.

"Next, he decided that he wanted a baby and I told him that with the problems we were having, we shouldn't bring a baby into it. There was anger, hostility and, of course, the depressing feeling that somewhere in my life I had made such a terrible mistake that it would take only God to fix it. I had to get out of this relationship because it was draining the life out of me. I decided to tell him that I wanted a divorce. Well, again, all hell broke loose. He told me he would never divorce me, that he loved me. That he would do whatever necessary to change and he was sorry for all the pain he had caused me. 'Please don't leave!' he cried. 'Things will change!' I didn't believe him, but I still stayed. You really want to believe that maybe things will change.

"Everything was good for about three more months, until I came home and found another woman in my house and Harold drunk. This man told me that he was putting me out of my own house, a house that I bought. He had packed my things and told me that I was old and he didn't want me anymore, that he had a young woman. Someone he could show off to his friends.

"Well, I looked at them both and lost it. I had to stop and pull myself together. I went to the phone and called the police. When they got there, I told them I wanted them to escort everybody out of my house whose name wasn't on the deed. Did he think that I was going to leave MY house? It's amazing that when a man feels that he doesn't want you anymore, that you are too old, he wants to get rid of you for some young girl born yesterday.

"After divorcing Harold, I finally had happiness back. But it didn't last long. I so desperately wanted to love and have someone to return that love. I wanted that perfect relationship. One year later, I settled again and married Richard. I should have gotten to know him better before I married him. The minute we said, 'I do,' things changed.

"He was another non-ideal husband. I found out that Richard had issues with hygiene and living habits. He didn't like to wash his behind and I hardly ever saw him brush his teeth. I had to argue with him to go to the dentist. Once, his breath was so bad I told him that he should see a dentist. He told me that he was around people all the time and no one had ever told him that he had bad breath. I wondered what had I gotten myself into.

"He would wear the same underwear for days and there was a washing machine and dryer in the house. I was always washing and buying new underclothes for him. He didn't care. We had separate bedrooms; I wouldn't let him touch me.

"He didn't want to work and he didn't. Every job he got, he couldn't keep. He couldn't hold down a job if you tied him to it and he would change jobs as often as I change the sheets. He was not reliable; I was responsible for everything. When I would confront him about his inability to do anything he would curse me out. He wanted me to take care of him, told me that I made enough money to take care of us both. I had to hide my purse, credit cards and bankbook. He even went to the bank to try and get money out and had the nerve to tell the teller that he had a right to the money because he was my husband.

"He would put me down in front of my friends and treated me as if I were stupid. Then, he started to physically abuse me. I wasn't going to let that happen, so I pulled a gun on him and told him I would blow his brains out if he ever hit me again.

"I was letting this man change me into something I was not, and didn't want to be. The relationship was long dead and if it didn't end, one or both of us was going to be also. I was so lonely for love that I didn't take the time to get to know Richard and his nasty self. I honestly thought I loved this man.

"Once my marriage was dead with Richard, I wanted him gone. Ladies, I was praying for another woman to take him right out of my life! 'Please, God,' I prayed, 'I don't want anything bad to happen to him and he won't leave, so please let him find someone else.' Now I didn't want to wish his sorry behind on some other woman, but he was hanging out with other women anyway; maybe one of them would take him.

"This man was having the friends he hung out with come to our house all hours of the night and they would sit and talk all night long about the women they had, with no regards to me being in the next room. I was wondering what type of women would be with these men. But then it came to me, 'A woman like you.'

"I had to get myself out of this situation. I had settled. There had to be a man out there who wants everything I am: smart, loving, caring, educated and clean. I was sure there was, but figured most likely he was already dating or in a wonderful relationship. Richard had no respect for me at all, and I had none for him. When you lose respect for your mate, I believe it is time to go; all that is left is the ending.

"I had experienced Richard at his worse. His ways had become conniving and hateful. He was a liar and a cheater. I was fed up with him. He had done many nasty things to me. I wasn't going to take it anymore. There was no compassion, no trust, no faith and certainly no love left; he had to go. When you are abused and disrespected daily, you ask yourself, 'Why am I here?' I had had enough and was starting to think of things to get even with him, but God intervened and I knew I had to leave him.

"I told him he was not a man but an insecure, self-centered freak and he didn't deserve my love. I told him I wanted a divorce and I was seeing a lawyer the next day. He threatened me. I knew I had to be careful how I handled this, because a man like this will kill you.

"Why is it that when you tell a man the relationship is over, he starts to change right there in front of your eyes? He cried and told me how sorry he was; and he went and got a job and started to do things I had never seen him do before. He became clean overnight, started washing himself and went to the dentist. He started going to church and begged me to please stay with him and said that he was willing to get counseling. He was so insecure. Insecure men are the most toxic and if they are afraid you are going to leave them, they will find a way to hang onto you, no matter what they have done to you. But he wasn't paying attention to what I was telling him. I had to tell him that my love for him had died and no matter what he did, it could never be rekindled because my heart and soul had been so abused by him. I felt nothing for him anymore.

"Men don't understand that when a woman is fed up there isn't anything they can do about it. They just got to get to stepping. I was beginning to hate him. I had never felt that way about anybody—and this man was my husband. When he would try to hold me or kiss me, I would turn away with disgust. He told me that he wasn't going to let me leave him and that if I wanted the marriage to end that I would have to be the one to leave. I packed his bags and told him he had to leave my house—and if he didn't, I was going to have to go to the authorities. History was repeating itself.

"You see, Briana, I was out there looking for the perfect man. Well, let me tell you, perfect isn't out there. We all come with imperfections, but there is always a right man for us and we can be the right woman for that man, if we make ourselves so. Imperfect people can create the perfect relationship.

"Once again, I was divorced, all by myself, lonely. But I had rather be by myself and lonely than to go through what I had gone through with the marriages I had.

"I found myself thinking about Robert. It was my fault we had separated. I was so young when we married. When I was married to him, I loved him so much that I wanted to do everything for him. I was a control freak and lost the man I knew I could have been happy with. I began to look back over my life and the dead–end relationships from my past. I started to wonder if God wanted me to be happy in marriage. Suddenly, something clicked. I thought, 'Why do I want marriage so badly when it cannot provide me the unconditional love my heart craves? Only God can give me everything I need!' And so, with this, I gave everything to Christ. I relinquished to Him my demand to have a husband. I was hopeful that someday I would find my Mr. Right, but I wasn't going to consider it necessary to make me happy. I decided if I remained single for the rest of my life, that I would be fine. And from then on, the men I would date would have to be like Christ. Jesus likes me, He loves me and He keeps me.

"My life started to take on a whole new meaning. I was happy. I wasn't even dating. I had a good church family and was enjoying the relationship I was having with the new man in my life, Jesus. What a friend He is. I embedded in my brain that God is in control of everything, that no matter what we are going through, He won't intervene just to make our lives easy. That He would not magically make a man appear and fall madly in love with me. Instead God gave me the sense of knowing that when the time was right, He would give me a husband and I would have the unconditional love that He gives to us. All I had to do is wait on Him. With Him controlling my life, I had no worries at all. I was happy with the way my life was going. And then, something wonderful happened.

"I was shopping downtown one day when I heard someone calling my name. It was Robert! I was happy to see him and he seemed happy to see me. He said he had heard that I was divorced; I told him I was. He asked me out to dinner and that was the beginning of the rest of my life. I wasn't looking for anybody and out of the blue, Robert found me. He found me! My mother always told my sister and me that we don't have to go looking for a husband, that God will send him and that he will find us. For the first time in years, I was happy again. I was going to make sure this time that I didn't mess things up.

"Robert told me that he knew I was the right woman for him the first time he met me. He said I changed when we got married and became controlling and dominating but he loved me so much he was willing to stay with me and hoped I would change. He said that even then, he didn't think that there was, or that there ever could be, anyone better than me out there for him. But as the marriage progressed, I wouldn't listen to him and just took over. He wasn't mature enough to handle the situation so he left. We got divorced and went our separate ways. He told me that he dated several women, but didn't find anyone he could commit to. He was looking for someone like me, but without being controlling.

"We were so happy to have found each other again. After several dates, he told me that I wasn't the woman he had divorced, that I was the woman he had fallen in love with a long time ago, not the controlling wife he had left. He said that when he heard I was divorced, he knew he shouldn't have been, but he was happy because he could now come to me and maybe we could start all over again.

"I find it amazing that we both were right for each other the first time we were married, but we made ourselves into the wrong mates for each other. If only I had known how to have made myself the perfect wife for Robert, I wouldn't have gone through what I did with Harold and Richard.

"We saw each other almost every day after that; we took our time and got to know each other all over again. We talked about what we wanted in a relationship, in a marriage. We were able to put everything about what we liked or did not like about our past marriage on the table. We decided that we were right for each other and started making plans to remarry. But first, we promised each other that we would be patient with each other's weaknesses and faults. We would not point out each other's faults over and over—and that I would deal with his faults the way I would want him to deal with mine.

"Briana, Robert was the prefect man for me from the first time I had met him. I was the one who had messed up. I thought he wanted me to do the things I was doing in the marriage. My mother was that way with my father, but my father wanted her to take care of everything. Instead of talking to Robert when he tried to talk to me about it, I wouldn't listen to him and lost him. He was the right man for me, but I made myself the wrong woman for him. When I let go of what I was, I became what I should have been and received what I needed.

"You need to think about the reason you won't marry Josiah. And really, it's none of our business. But don't lose out on happiness because your husband has to be Black. If you feel that you are right for each other, you love each other, respect each other and are honest with each other, what else is there, but to commit to each other? Please don't let Josiah's race keep you from happiness. Love has always been the greatest emotional risk. We risk our souls and hearts; we get so wrapped up in it. Our entire beings get lost in it. We know that love can hurt us more than any human emotion and yet, everyone wants it and needs it. We thrive on it.

"In your case, love knocked at your door when you weren't even expecting it. Josiah came knocking and told you he wants to marry you. With him being white, you didn't know what to do and ran. You have this wonderful man in your life who has told you that he loves you and wants to marry you. Do you leave it, put it on hold to see if you can find your Black prince charming, or do you take it? I would much rather prefer a true attempt at creating a lasting intimacy and seeing it through for what it's worth than neglecting to do so because the man is not Black. You don't want to marry Josiah, yet you want to hold on to him. How long do you think he is going to wait on you? You need to think about what you are doing to him, his feelings. If you love him, go ahead and take the chance. Believe me, there is nothing more satisfying than loving someone who loves you back. Love exists for all of us in one form or another. It is truly what gives being human any real significance at the end of the day.

"There may be a Black man out there for you. If that's what you want, I wish you nothing but the best. It took me fifteen years to finally find happiness, to get the perfect relationship. All those years I wasted on the wrong men.

"You know some people can have all the luck when it comes to finding love, while others like me have to work a little bit harder. I've always believed that there is someone who was created just made for you. And I also believe that we sometimes have to go through rough patches to achieve our dreams and happiness. God knows I have gone through mine—and maybe a lot of somebody else's.

"I always had in mind what I thought the perfect marriage would be, and once I had found that special person to share it with, I was going to execute my plan with perfection and have the marriage of a lifetime. Well, after a few mishaps, I finally found someone that I am happy with, after all these years, after going through two failed relationships. I finally get it. It's all about trust. Sweetie, you only live once; you said yourself that you love Josiah. Don't let love slip past you because he is not Black. You can have your own thoughts about a relationship, but the truth of it is you are either going to go with what it takes to learn more about yourself and how you relate to others and learn from your past involvements, or you will continue to walk around in denial thinking you are right and the rest of us are wrong.

"Right now, I can't imagine my life any differently, but despite all the pain I had been through, I was still open to love and giving it, another try with someone I had been married to before, regardless of whatever shortcomings I had in our past relationship. You only live one life, and nothing compares to having that one person in your life who loves you with all his being and you are right there to give it right back to him, taking a chance on love. If I were you, I would make myself open and take a chance on him. But I am not you. Ask yourself if he loves you. Do you trust him? Whatever answer you come up with, I think you will know what to do.

"I am not telling you what to do. I just don't want you to go through what I did with men who didn't give a damn about me. Fifteen years is a long time to be with the wrong man, to be unhappy, especially when you had the right man all along and let him slip away. Look, all I am saying is that the relationships I had with the Mr. Wrongs in my life didn't have to be. You have a man in your life that you love and you know he loves you and wants to marry you. But because he is white, you want to put him aside to see if you can find a Black man that has the same qualities that this man has. I am not saying that there isn't a Black man out there that will have these qualities, because there is, but do you think you will find him tomorrow?

"How long will you keep Josiah waiting before he says to hell with it and moves on. If Robert were white would I have married him? Well, if he loved me like the Black Robert does, treated me like a queen like my Black Robert does and once a month makes it a habit to go out on a date where he surprises me with something special.. Yes, I would marry him. When it comes to my Robert, does he love me? Damn right, he does. This man loves me. And I love him right back. Black or white, I would love this man.

"Remember our motto poem? My favorite verse is:

'Love is enjoyable, pleasing and nice
Some like it so much they tried it twice!
You are my lover, my dream come true
Forever and ever I will love you!'"

Melody was young when she married Robert and believed she was doing what was best for her marriage. She thought she had to be in charge like her mother was with her father. She could have saved her marriage with Robert and had the perfect relationship if only she had listened to him, communicated with him. This would have spared her the heartache she had with her two other husbands.

There are some of us who need and want love so badly that we mess up our own lives and end up being in unhealthy relationships that are controlling, abusive and disrespectful. I am sure the signs are there before you are hardly into the relationship. Maybe he yelled at you, insulted you; put you down in front of others. Maybe he showed signs that he would let himself go and neglect his personal hygiene or refuse to clean up behind himself.

Heartache could have been spared if Melody had gotten to know Harold and Richard before rushing into the marriages thinking maybe she could change them. She knew she couldn't trust them, yet she married them anyway. It's easy to fall in love with a man you don't trust, but it's hard to live with him.

Chapter 8

Kayla

Briana came over to sit beside me. "Kayla, it seems that everyone here has said something but you. You and Elijah have been married for twenty years; you seem to still be so much in love with each other. What is your opinion? How did you two meet and how did you know he was the one? What have you to say about my relationship with Josiah?"

I will not tell you to marry Josiah or not to marry him. Only you can decide that. But I will tell you a little about love and happiness.

"When I first met Elijah, I cannot to this day describe how I felt. I had never had this feeling before and it scared me. I fell in love with him the minute we met. When he came into my life, I knew he was the one. He was dating someone else and didn't even know I existed. I knew he someday would be my husband and I even told one of my co-workers that I was going to marry him. She looked at me and said, 'Please, he has been dating his girlfriend for three years, they are inseparable.' I told her that I didn't care about that. I was going to be Mrs. Elijah Wilson.

"I had an interview for a great job at a bank in Virginia Beach when I met Elijah. He was the director of the personnel department.

"When I went into his office for my interview, I had no idea that the man I was about to meet would change my life forever and make me the happiest woman in the world.

THE PERFECT RELATIONSHIP

"I was so nervous. There was something about him. I felt a connection. I knew he was my destiny. Right at that moment, I knew I was looking at my husband. I sat down across from him and when I looked in his face, my heart skipped a beat. My blood rushed to my face. My eyesight became blurred. The room became dark; for a moment, I thought it was midnight, but I knew it was morning. And the way he smelled will forever remain in my nostrils. When he spoke to me, my heart almost stopped, his voice was so seductive. All he said was, 'Good morning, Miss Boone, I am Elijah Wilson. Will you please come into my office? Have a seat, please.' I was in love from that moment on. I thought I was going to pass out. I was happy to be sitting. I was sweating buckets and was having trouble focusing. I started to pray.

"Dear God, please bring me back to my senses. Don't let me make a fool of myself in front of this man. And God, while I am praying, Thank You! Thank You! Thank You!' Once in a lifetime, you find someone special, your lives become intermingled and somehow you know that this is the person that God has placed in your life.

"Some of us are lucky to have a miracle happen the first time we meet the person we know will be our soul mate. And I say this to you because it happened to me. I knew Elijah was my soul mate. I knew because my heart was telling me, and my instincts.

"Now at that time in my life, I wasn't looking for anybody. I was twenty-five and just finished getting my Master's degree. I was content with and in my life. I had found myself. I knew who I was, what my aspirations and dreams were. I knew what sort of qualities it took from others to make me happy. I was truly happy with myself and by myself.

"I was hired by Elijah as manager in the Mutual Funds Department. He welcomed me aboard and took me down to the floor I would be working on and introduced me to the people I would be working with. One of them was Miss Thelma Darden, his fiancée. She was attractive, tall and had a nice figure. I mean she was beautiful. She looked like Halle Berry, but when she turned around, it was Jennifer Lopez.

"Later, when I went to the bathroom, I looked at myself in the full-length mirror. 'Now,' I said to myself, 'I am just as attractive as she is.' That was from the neck up. Below the neck down, I was a size four and skinny. Miss Thelma had it going on.

"Did that bother me, NO! The minute I walked into Elijah's office and he shook my hand, I knew he was mine. I could feel it from the tip of my head to the bottom of my feet. My whole body, my soul had become drunk with him.

"For three weeks, I worked closely with Thelma as she trained me. She was very nice. We liked each other and when she wasn't having lunch with Elijah, we would have lunch together. Even though they had set a wedding date, I still wasn't worried about Elijah becoming my husband. I knew he would be.

"I would go home and pray. My prayers to God were, 'God, I know You are in control of my life and I give it all to You. Now I am not questioning Your reasons, but why are You punishing me? You told me that Elijah is my soul mate. What's going on here?' His answer was to wait. I have a very good rapport with God and I talk to Him like I talk to all of you. He's my friend, He understands me. So, I waited. When you know that God is telling you something, you listen and then you are obedient.

"I never approached Elijah as no more than being my boss. He had no idea how I felt or I thought; he didn't. I went to work each day just to see him. Now I did my job, and did it well. I dressed very nicely, made sure my hair and nails were always well groomed. I made sure I looked good, even Thelma complimented me. I would catch Elijah looking, but he was always a gentleman. Every man on the job was trying to get my attention but him.

"One morning, I heard him talking to Thelma that his mother's birthday was in a few days and if she had the time, to pick up some Red Door perfume for her, that it was her favorite. Thelma tried to get him to buy something else, telling him that she herself didn't like Red Door, but he insisted that she purchase it, saying his mother liked Elizabeth Arden and he liked it, also.

"On my lunch hour, I ran to Macy's to buy some for me. I prayed about that also. 'God, please forgive me, it's only perfume.' When I wore it, he noticed and told me it was his mother's favorite. Thelma heard and came over later to tell me that Elijah made her sick when it came to his mother. I knew then that something was wrong with the relationship, but I kept my distance.

"Three weeks later at the Christmas party, I overheard Thelma tell one of our co-workers that she would meet him in five minutes in her office. Unbeknownst to her, Elijah had heard it also and had followed her. The following Monday, she told me that their engagement was off and she had given him the ring back. Now you know I wanted to shout for joy, but that would have been wrong. But I did pray silently, right there in front of her. I said in my mind, 'Thank You, Lord. THANK YOU.'

"Later at home, I went to God in prayer. 'Heavenly Father, it's me again. I come to You to ask that You forgive me for being happy that Elijah and Thelma have broken up, because when a couple is engaged and breaks up, someone gets hurt. But, Lord, you told me that this man is going to be my husband and I truly believe You, so this was supposed to happen. Lord, I believe this man is for me and I am praying that You will let him see that he and I are meant to be.' I then asked God for guidance, for both of us, and that He would direct Elijah to me. Some may think it is wrong to ask God for a man. I wasn't asking God for a man. I was praying for my man, my intended husband-to-be.

"The following week, Elijah and I had to work very closely together on a project that Thelma was supposed to do. She surprised us all; she resigned and relocated to New York. God was answering my prayers.

"Elijah and I worked well together and before I knew it, we were having lunch together. He still didn't know how I felt. I wanted him to notice me as more than a co-worker, more than a friend to have lunch with. When this didn't happen, I decided to not have lunch with him anymore. I would avoid him. If I was waiting for the elevator and he was on it when it stopped, I would wait for another one. If I went into the lunchroom and saw him, I would turn around and leave. Once, at a staff meeting, he came in and sat beside me, I got up and moved. Now I wasn't doing these things on purpose. I liked him so much that I was avoiding being hurt.

"I still prayed for us, but I changed it. You have to be careful how you pray; you have to be specific in the things you ask for. I started praying that Elijah would see me as more than a co-worker and that he would see me as a mate, a wife. God was telling me to be still and wait. And that is what I did. You must learn to wait on God. You must be in a habit of praying and having faith that He is going to answer your prayers.

"Things now were beginning to change. I was seeing signs that Elijah was interested in me. I kept my distance on the job. At home, I was taking extra care to pick out my clothes at night and stocked up on Elizabeth Arden's Red Door, making sure that when he saw me, he would not only smell his mother's favorite scent, but that he would want to be near me.

THE PERFECT RELATIONSHIP

"Back then, people used to tell me that I looked like a model and walked like one. Well, I would walk past Elijah making sure he was close enough to smell me, and as I passed him, I would say, 'Good morning, Mr. Wilson,' or 'Good afternoon, Mr. Wilson,' depending on the time of day it was. I would do my model walk. I was setting him up. Now, I can't say if that was the right thing to do, but I think that if God is telling you that someone is your future husband, that you have to help it along a little. As long as you don't go overboard with it and scare him away.

"One morning in March, I was getting out of my car when Elijah drove up and parked next to me. I spoke to him and kept on walking. As I reached the entrance to the building, he had caught up with me. He called out to me, 'Kayla, wait. Are you avoiding me?' Before I could answer, he said, 'You look very pretty today. If you haven't any plans for lunch, will you have lunch with me?' I told him that I wouldn't have time to; I had a new employee to train. I didn't want to seem anxious. He kept pleading, 'Please have lunch with me.' I told him I would and he said, 'I'll meet you here at 12 noon.'

"At noon, when I got to the main floor, he was standing there waiting for me. We went to this nice restaurant three blocks from the bank. We had a nice time; we got to know a little more about each other and he asked me if I would go out with him Saturday. I told him that I would be busy most of Saturday with my sister, but if it was okay we could have a late dinner. I gave him my sister's number and told him he could call me there after four. I was so excited. Things were finally getting to where I wanted them to be with him.

"Well, he never called me all weekend. I waited at my sister's house for the call. When he didn't call, I went home and told myself that it just wasn't going to be.

DR. CAROLYN WHITE-BROWN

"Monday morning, I didn't want to go to work. I didn't want to see Elijah. Well, he was the first person I saw standing by the elevator. I avoided him and walked up the stairs to my floor. When I got to my office he was standing there. I went off on him. 'Look, what do you want from me? I waited for you and you never called. Do me a favor and stay away from me!' I left him standing there.

"About an hour later, my secretary came into my office with a dozen red roses saying, 'These are for you.' I knew they had to be from Elijah. I told her she could have them. She said, 'Aren't you going to read the card to see who they are from?' I told her I knew who they were from and took them and threw them in the garbage can.

"About twenty minutes after that, Elijah called and wanted to know if I had received the flowers. I hung up on him. Ten minutes later my secretary buzzed me that Mr. Wilson was here to see me. I told her to tell him that I was busy.

"Before I knew what was happening, he was in my office. He came around to where I was sitting, pulled me up on my feet, took me in his arms and gave me a kiss that I can still feel to this day. I was speechless.

"He went into his wallet, took out a slip of paper and said, 'Is this the number you gave? Look at it,' he demanded. 'I tried to call you. I wanted to call you. This is a wrong number. You gave me a wrong number!'

"'I did not give you a wrong number!' I yelled back, 'Why would I do that?'

"I took the slip out of his hand. He was right, I was in such a hurry to give him the number, I wrote it down wrong. The last digit was off. I started to apologize, 'Elijah I am so sorry.' Before I could finish, he took me in his arms and kissed me again. This time, I kissed him back. I felt dizzy; a shiver ran down my spine. If I hadn't been in his arms, I would have fallen. Just to talk about that makes me weak in my knees now. I have to finish telling this sitting down!

"That was the beginning of the rest of my life. We had lunch that day and every day after. We were inseparable and in love. We started to ride to work together. He would pick me up in the morning and would be waiting for me after work to take me home.

"On weekends, we were together. We knew that we were meant to be. He told me that when I first came into his office that, even though he was engaged to Thelma, he was attracted to me; that he had to go to God in prayer to understand what was happening. How could he be engaged to one woman, planning marriage, and another woman walks into his office and takes his heart right there on the spot? He had thought Thelma was the one and they had become engaged. But she had changed on him and he had suspected her of cheating. When he overheard her planning to meet another man in her office during the Christmas party, he followed her and caught her kissing him. He broke off the engagement right then.

"He told me that when he saw me sitting in the waiting area, there was an attraction. And when the interview was over and he took me down to my floor, that he couldn't keep his eyes off me, that he loved the way I talked, the way I walked. He said that he honestly thought Thelma was the one, but when I came along, he knew differently. He couldn't let me know his feelings, because he was with Thelma and he wasn't going to cheat on either one of us. So, he kept praying to God for guidance; and even after he had broken it off with Thelma, he wanted to pray about me to make sure I was the one. That is why he ignored me for a while. He was praying.

"Elijah told me that finding Mrs. Right is not so much about finding the perfect woman, because there isn't one. He said that Mrs. Right for any man may be the one who, like himself, is full of imperfections, but the two can still love and can be fulfilled if they are willing to work with each other's imperfections. He said that if you know what you want in a companion—outside of good looks and chemistry—you will be better equipped at finding that person and knowing what your expectations will be with that person.

"He told me that a man needs a woman who cares only for him, not what he has, how much money he makes or what kind of car he drives. He said a man needs a companion who will encourage and support him, dream with him; someone who will bring out the best in him. He said that men need to know that no matter what they see when they look in the mirror, that their woman will see them as the smartest and the most irresistible man on the face of the earth.

"Then he took me in his arms and said, 'Kayla, every man needs a woman like you. You are my dream come true. I am so blessed to have found you.'

"During my teenage years, I had dreamed about what my husband would look like, be like. And as a young woman, God had given him to me. He was everything I had hoped for.

"Ladies, I loved this man. We continued to date. Before I knew it, he was talking about taking me to meet his family.

"When I met his parents for the first time, I got along well with them. His mother told me that she had heard so much about me, and wondered when Elijah was going to bring me to meet her. When it was time for us to leave, his mother told me that she was happy to meet me and that she was looking forward to me being her daughter-in-law. That took me by surprise. Had Elijah been talking to her about marriage? Then she took my hand and said, 'Kayla, you remind me so much of me when I was a young girl. Please come back to see me soon.' His mother and I became friends before Elijah and I were married. She was such a good mother-in-law. My father-in-law was just as nice. My in-laws, may they rest in peace, were terrific.

"The following Sunday, Elijah and I went to church. We both belonged to different churches, so we would rotate churches. This Sunday, we went to his church. He sang in the choir, usually he was the soloist. This Sunday, as he was singing, he started to walk down from the choir stand. He continued singing down the aisle right to the back of the church. I had my eyes closed, feeling the song, when I felt someone taking my hand. I opened my eyes. It was Elijah. I looked to see what was going on. All the choir members were standing down the aisle and he asked me to stand. He ended the song and right there, in front of everyone; he got down on his knee, took a ring box out of his pocket, opened it and asked me to marry him. I knew that he would propose, but I was totally caught off guard. Before I could answer, he started to sing Endless Love, but he changed the words around. I still remember the words he sang:

"Kayla, there's only you in my life. I want you to be my wife.'

"I started to cry. I was a mess. People were clapping and some were saying, 'You better tell him yes. Tell him yes!' I pulled myself together long enough to say yes and then I was back to the ugly cry.

"Everyone was so excited. The pastor said, 'Well, ladies she said yes. That means that Elijah is no longer available, so stay out of his face. And church, looks like there is going to be a wedding soon.'

"I couldn't stop looking at my ring. Now I know this is wrong, but the first thing I did was look at my ring to make sure it wasn't the same one Thelma had. You all know I had checked it out when she and Elijah were engaged. God, please forgive me for that! But it wasn't the same ring. Elijah must have sensed my concern, because later at dinner at his parents', he said, 'I saw you examining the ring. Kayla, I love you. I want you to know you are my lady, the only one that I truly love. I wouldn't have given you Thelma's ring. That would have been an insult to you. Thelma did give it back. I exchanged it for the one I gave you. You are, and always will be, first in my life. You deserve the best and if you will continue to love me and trust me I will, with God's help, give you the best there is to give.'

"Our wedding was small, about one hundred people. My sister made my dress. My father was ill and couldn't come. My oldest brother gave me away. It was very beautiful. We honeymooned in the Bahamas.

"Briana, my situation was so much different than yours. I saw Elijah and knew from that moment that I wanted to marry him. You have dated Josiah for over a year and you don't know if you want to marry him—and the only reason you have given is he's White and you have to marry a Black man. One minute, you tell us that you love this guy and he makes you happy, that what you feel with him is like nothing you have felt with the other men you dated. Now when he wants to commit and tells you that he wants to take it a step further and marry you, you run. If you truly love him, then his race shouldn't matter. We go through life risking our hearts and souls for love. It affects our minds, sometimes our entire being. Elijah took my heart the minute I laid eyes on him. When love takes its hold on us—if it is good, and the other person loves us back—we experience an incredible gift. If it doesn't work out, we then curse it and hate it for all the pain and hurt it caused.

"All of us who have found love and are in search of love must know and recognize that love will hurt us more than any other human emotion. To love another, requires a lot of spirit and we must have the strength to take on whatever comes with it. As Jerry Butler sang, only the strong survive.

"I think you should go to God in prayer and ask Him for guidance. I feel that the most important relationship any of us have is our personal relationship with Him. If your relationship with Him is as it should be, all else will fall into place.

"If you can't make up your mind about Josiah, ask yourself if you can trust each other, if you both respect each other, then this should be considered. Ask yourself why you were attracted to him in the beginning: physical attraction, similar interests, desire for children. And then ask yourself if you think you would want to live with this man in a marriage for the rest of your life.

"You know, Briana, my marriage is not a perfect marriage, but it is an exceptionally good marriage—a happy marriage, a fulfilling marriage.

"There are imperfections. I found out after we were married that Elijah snores, chews with his mouth open and he farts loud in my presence. Right now, I sleep on the side of the bed closest to the door. I tell him that he is supposed to sleep there, because if someone were to come in, he would be able to protect me. He tells me that he cannot sleep on that side. Now, when we are on vacation, staying in hotels, he sleeps on the side where the door is because he says if anyone comes in, he will be there to protect me. The first time he did this, I asked him the difference between protecting me at home and in a hotel. He said that at home is different because we have an alarm system, LOL.

"He mixes peas and rice with mayo. I hate it, but when he asks me to fix it for him, I do. Now I hog all the hot water; he tells me that I shower too long. I hang my underwear all over the bathroom. I complain that the air conditioner is up too high. I like to have the radio on while I am in bed, listening to love songs. He like sports, I don't. When we are at home relaxing, I have these old raggedy pajamas that I love and he hates. My hair is in rollers, which he hates.

"Usually, we are watching television in separate rooms, but we come together at bedtime and pray together as husband and wife. Before we go to sleep, we ask for God's protection over our home, our children and each member of our family. We ask God for continuous blessings in our marriage and that we continue to be loving, sensitive and helpful to each other.

"Before we were married, he took my breath away; now after twenty years of marriage, I feel sometimes like I am suffocating. He tells me that when we first got married, I wore Victoria's Secret all the time, now it's no name brands!

"He came up behind me once when I was cooking and whispered in my ear to come upstairs early. I leaned back into him and softly asked him why. He said he had a surprise for me. I knew exactly what it was. I hurried with what I was doing.

"Finally, the kids were in bed. I took a nice bubble bath in the body wash he gave me for Christmas and put on my sexiest nightgown. He was in bed waiting for me. We forgot all about the children.

THE PERFECT RELATIONSHIP

"Suddenly there was a loud knock on the door, a man's voice calling, "Mr. Wilson, this is the police. Come out with your hands up.' Elijah called out, 'It's who? What do you want?' The police answered back, "Mr. Wilson if you don't open this door, we are going to break it down!"

"Well, Elijah jumped up, put on his robe and opened the door. Before he could say anything, they pulled him out.

"Where is your wife?' they demanded. I was still in bed with the covers pulled up to my neck.

"She's in the bedroom! Why, what is going on?'

"I quickly put on my robe and rushed to see what was going on. There were policemen everywhere. 'Officers, what seems to be the problem?' I asked. They all looked at me.

"Mrs. Wilson, are you, all right?' Of course, why are you in my house?'

"We received a 911 call from your children that their father was killing their mother. They heard you screaming and calling on the Lord to help you."

"Elijah and I looked at each other. There was a woman officer with them. I pulled her to the side and explained to her what had been going on. She went over and whispered to one of the officers who was holding Elijah. He turned him loose and had to turn his face to keep from laughing.

"Where are my children?' I asked.

"We have them outside in one of the cars. When we got the call, we told them to quietly come downstairs and wait for us on the porch.'

"I ran down the stairs so my children could see I was alright. Imagine explaining this to an eleven-, ten- and seven-year-old.

"In a marriage, you never know what is going to happen next. When going out, I am slow; he has to wait for me. He is always on time. Now, are we going to divorce because of our differences and all the other stuff that comes along with it? No. This is married life.

"When you have found the person, you feel you want to marry, decide what you can live with and imagine yourself sitting with your fat, toothless, bald husband at the dinner table the rest of your life. Now he is going to imagine the same about you.

"When you met, you were young, had a nice figure; always well groomed. Now after having the babies, you have gained a little weight. The cute little bikini panties and bra set you used to wear have turned into large bloomers and 18-hour bras; your hair is turning grey and both of you are putting your teeth in water for the night.

"If you feel that you can live with each other till death do you part because your thoughtfulness and love for each other is greater than all that, then you know that you have found the right person for you.

"My marriage to Elijah is about friendship and a partnership that is honest, supportive and friendly. He makes me feel protected. When I turn over in bed and he's there, I know there is nothing to worry about. He's there for me. We have respect for each other most of the time. Sometimes something may happen that we may disrespect each other, but out of respect, it's only in our mind, never openly. We fight rarely, regardless of the situation and we have a lot of fun enjoying each other's company. He will wash my hair if I ask him to and I will do his feet, massage and pedicure, if he asks me to. Sometimes when he is in the shower, I will sneak in and pour cold water

THE PERFECT RELATIONSHIP

over him and try to get out before he can catch me. If he catches me, he pulls me in the shower getting my clothes and hair all wet. We end up completing the shower together and making love for the rest of the evening.

"Now after twenty years of marriage, the love making has changed some also. When we were first married, it was new. We used to try to devour each other, and we never got enough. We would make love twenty times a month. Now it's maybe five times a month. But, also, we have learned to satisfy each other differently. We take our time, and tell each other what we'd like for the other one to do. As newlyweds, it lasted twenty minutes. Now it's forty-five minutes to an hour. It really doesn't matter how long it is, as long as it is satisfying. You all have heard the Pointer Sisters' song, Slow Hand. Well, after being married twenty years, a slow hand is fantastic.

"We are comfortable with each other. I wouldn't change a thing. There's no secret to our marriage, we just do what is needed for each other. That's what a perfect relationship is. I can't imagine myself being married to any other man but Elijah and I do my best to keep him happy.

"When we were first married, we had my parents over for dinner. After dinner, my mother told me that she liked Elijah a lot and that she could tell that he really loved me. She said, 'He likes to touch you and his hands are all over you, pulling you closer and kissing you.' She went on to say, 'Baby, if your husband likes to be all over you, please don't get tired of it. A man like that is truly in love with his woman, craves the nearness of her. And if you get tired of him doing that and start pushing him away, he will look for it someplace else. When it comes to your husband, you can't have other women outdoing you for his love, his touches.'

"I have never forgotten that. Elijah, to this day, still likes to touch and is always pulling me to him whether at home or in public. I love it, and other women have noticed it and have commented on it. Some tell me that they wish their husbands were as affectionate.

"I give my husband my all. I tell him I love him often. I treat him like the king he is. I always compliment him. Whatever he does for me, I let him know that I appreciate it. I tell him I don't know what I would do without him.

"If we have an argument, we make an effort to not get so upset that we may say something that we may regret later. One of us will say, 'Stop, let's take a break.' This gives us time to calm down. Later we sit down and talk it out. We each listen to what the other has to say. If I am wrong, I will tell him and vice versa. We then make up. We never go to bed angry. +

"We respect each other, are committed, communicate well, and are faithful, honest and true. We love each other with all our hearts. We are both Christians and believe that God brought us together.

"Our marriage is full of romance. We are not ashamed to love each other in intimacy. As husband and wife, God has given us this marriage as a gift. The book of Song of Solomon tells us that we honor God when we love and enjoy each other. One of my favorite scriptures in Song of Solomon is 8:6-7. It reads, 'Place me like a seal over your heart, like a seal on your arm; for love is as strong as death, its jealousy unyielding as the grave. It burns like blazing fire, like a mighty flame. Many waters cannot quench love; rivers cannot sweep it away. If one were to give all the wealth of one's house for love, it would be utterly scorned.'

"My study Bible interpreted this as meaning love is as strong as death; it cannot be killed by time or disaster and it cannot be bought for any price because it is freely given. Love is priceless and even the richest king cannot buy it. Love must be accepted as a gift from God and then shared within the guidelines God provides. It states we should accept the love of our spouse as God's gift, and strive to make our love a reflection of the perfect love that comes from God.

"You and Josiah are not married, but you love each other. He is willing to marry you, but you won't marry him. Briana, you have to go to God and ask Him for guidance. He will speak to your heart and He will let you know if Josiah is the right one for you or if you should wait for your black prince charming to come along.

"I am not sure because I have not experienced it, but I would think that people who back away from having an interracial marriage may have a deep-rooted stigma, meaning that this is not acceptable, or your subconscious is telling you that you should marry a black man.

"I have a cousin who is always being asked out by white men. She is dark skinned and is quite beautiful. She feels that if she were ugly they wouldn't have approached her. She thinks that they want to see what it is like to date and have sex with a beautiful black woman. Now she is very intelligent, a professor at Old Dominion University. But she is so hung up on the history of the white slave master's treatment of his female slaves that she thinks white men just want to use black women, that one could never be serious about her. What she doesn't realize is that if she were ugly, black men wouldn't ask her out either.

"My sister used to date a white man when she was in college at Harvard. She said he was nice, but became possessive and paranoid. If she wasn't home when he called, he would accuse her of being with another man. She broke it off with him and he didn't want to let go. When she would come back to her dormitory, he would be waiting for her. She had a hard time getting rid of him. He didn't understand what, 'No I don't want you,' meant. It ended when she finished college and moved back to Virginia.

"White men are no different than Black men. There are idiots in both races, there are abusive ones in both races and there are kind and loving ones in both races.

"I believe that when you are dating or attracted to someone, love conquers all. But because the other person is not from your race, we subconsciously eliminate them.

"If Elijah was white, would I have married him? I don't think I would have walked into his office and fell head over hills in love with him. I don't think I would have given him another thought. He would have had to make the first move and I can't say if I would have gone out with him if he had asked me.

"Maybe because Josiah is white you feel that he may betray you, he may use you. You had a friendship with Tommy and you were romantically involved with Michael. Both men betrayed you. Betrayal is an important motivator to not put your heart on the line again.

"Briana, love creates both happiness and heartache. The truth is that there really is no way to say for sure whether you and Josiah are compatible for the long term. In the beginning, everything seems to come easy. Sex is good, passion is high and you both are so busy trying to impress each other that you are going all out of your way to please each other. But you must understand that marriage changes things. Some of these things will be for the better and some for the worse. Remember the vows you will take: for better, for worse, in sickness and health, till death do us part.

"Not one of us in this room knew what it was going to be like down that road we were about to take when we got married.

THE PERFECT RELATIONSHIP

There were so many promises. My mother told me before I was married to make sure I could not live without Elijah, because you do not marry a person that you can live with, but rather you marry a person that you cannot live without.

"We all, whether married or not, have had our problems with the men in our lives. Some of us are still hanging in there while some had to let go. Marriage is scary. Just thinking that you will be committing yourself to one person for the rest of your life is something to think about.

"I never told any of you this, but on my wedding day, I had doubts. I knew I loved Elijah. But till death do us part we hope to be a long time. I was in the bride's waiting area sweating bullets. I was about to get out of there when my brother, Buddy, who was giving me away walked in and asked me where was I going. I told him I wasn't sure if I wanted to get married. He looked at me and said, 'So you are going to leave my man at the altar?' He took me by the arm and said, 'HELL NO. You told everybody how much you love this man. You had me to go and rent this tuxedo and as good as I look today, I am walking you down the aisle. Come on, they're playing your song.'

"Later, he would have us all laughing about it. Every time he told it, he would add more to it.

"When you love someone, really love someone, committing yourself to that person is the most valuable gift you can give.

"A good marriage takes work. When courting, and at the beginning of marriage, we feel our relationship will never have any problems. That it is always going to be like it was at the beginning. But over time, we soon learn that time changes us and we have to work at keeping things in order. Some of us work at it and some give up.

"It's your choice, Briana, whether you will take a chance on Josiah. Pray that God will lead you into making the right decision. He will lead you to the person most suitable for you. Just remember that even though loving is hard, it is beautiful no matter who you love. I think it was Alfred Lord Tennyson who said, 'I hold it true, whate'er befall; I feel it, when I sorrow most; 'Tis better to have loved and lost, than never to have loved at all.'

"Remember our poem? My favorite verse is:

'I thank you my love for being there
When I needed you the most?
Your caring heart has made me whole.
Your caring ways took over my soul.
You are my perfect love!'"

Briana stood up, "Ladies, you all are my friends and I really appreciate all your thoughts; and as you have all stated, the decision to marry Josiah is mine. I just think that there is a black man out there for me. I always saw myself with a black man having beautiful, black babies."

"So, what, if you end up having light-skinned babies? Would that be so bad? Would you love them differently?" Kima asked.

"I would love my children no matter what color they are."

"Briana, I hope you will be happy with whomever you choose for a husband," Marjorie commented. "I took a chance on Norman and haven't regretted one minute of it. Being a lawyer myself, I always thought I would marry a lawyer or a doctor, but that wasn't in God's plan. He gave me the husband I needed, not the one I wanted. Please, as we all have told you, go to Him in prayer, He will hear you and give you your heart's desire. You are afraid right now; you love this man, but you won't let go and let God. 2 Timothy 1:7 says, 'For God did not give us a spirit of timidity, but a spirit of power, of love and of self-discipline.' Whatever you do let God be in the midst of it. Psalms 127:1 says, 'Unless the Lord builds the house, its builders labor in vain. Unless the Lord watches over the city, the watchmen stand guard in vain.' Whomever you marry, we wish you nothing but love and happiness, whether he is Black or White."

"Amen to that!" shouted Kima. "I am sure there are a lot of decent brothers out there and one of them could be the right man for you and will treat you right; one that knows how to value a black woman on his arm, in public, in his home, in the bedroom and most importantly, in his heart. I know at least one brother like that. Just ask Michelle Obama."

With this, they all laughed. "Come on, let's eat, I am hungry!" Claudia said.

We always prayed before we ate. Briana prayed, "Heavenly Father, thank You for loving each of us. I ask You to bless my friends and family. Show them a new revelation of Your love and power. Thank You, Father, for the friendship you have given us. We thank You for giving us free will to love and ask forgiveness when we don't follow You and end up in broken relationships. Give us strength to do Your will. Guide our hearts to people that are worthy of our love and will give us the unconditional love you give to us.

Give us patience, love and kindness in how we interact with each other and our families. Bless us, O Lord, and this food, which we are about to receive through Thy bounty, Christ our Lord. Amen."

Author's Epilogue

What relationships these women had! Claudia, wife who did not divorce her husband; even after a violent beating she stayed with him.

Quiana discovered that communication is essential in a relationship. And you have to make the relationship a priority. She discovered that even if you lose your way for a period, it is possible to rekindle a love that is lost.

Camille and Carol, dealing with Down Low men and infidelity and husbands who wanted to stay with them because—even though they slept with men—they loved the women in their lives.

Kima, with a husband so immature that when the children came, he couldn't stand the attention she gave the babies; so, he went and found a woman who looked like his wife.

Few find a relationship like Marjorie, perfect and beautiful. She met a man who literally swept her off her feet—and she would have missed her perfect relationship if she had let job titles get in the way.

Briana finally decided that her desire to find a black partner was stronger than her attraction to Josiah. Sometimes we miss out on the perfect relationship by holding out for something we think might be better.

Melody should not have been so controlling in her first marriage. With honest communication, her relationship could have been saved and she could have avoided being married to two terrible men. Thank goodness, she found her way back to her first true love.

THE PERFECT RELATIONSHIP

Then there's Kayla. She knew from the moment she met Elijah that he was the right man for her. Even though he was engaged to someone else, she knew that she would marry him. How does someone get that much confidence to recognize their soul mate—even though he is dating someone else? She walked into Elijah's office and knew right away that he was the one.

A lot of us may have relationships like Quiana and Marjorie. All we have to do is communicate with each other and trust each other and the rest will fall in place.

For those who are in relationships with someone of another ethnic background, love has no color restrictions.

I am not a marriage analyst or expert at giving couples guidance on their relationships, but I do have over forty years' experience in being a happily married woman...most of the time. I know that making a good relationship is a job. We come to love not by finding a perfect person, but by learning to see an imperfect person perfectly.

You do not marry a person that you can live with, but rather you marry a person that you cannot live without. Thank you, Mama, for that one

And finally, let us talk about love. How deep is your love, anyway? Loving someone is not about getting what you want from a person, but rather what makes you happy when you give something to them.

Life has its ups and downs and married life seems to have more of them than single life.

All the couples were unique. Some found true everlasting love and marriage while some ended up in failed relationships.

Let us all remember what 1 Corinthians 13:4-10 tells us:

"Love is patient, love is kind. It does not envy, it does not boast, it is not proud. It is not rude, it is not self-seeking, it is not easily angered, it keeps no record of wrongs. Love does not delight in evil but rejoices with the truth. It always protects, always trusts, always hopes and always perseveres.

"Love never fails. But where there are prophecies, they will cease; where there are tongues, they will be stilled; where there is knowledge, it will pass away. For we know in part and we prophesy in part, but when perfection comes, the imperfect disappears."

May you all find everlasting love.

About the Author

Dr. Carolyn White-Brown was born and raised in Whaleyville Virginia. She is the mother of three children. Carol Allen And Todd. Grandmother of nine and great grandmother of six. She was married to Elijah her late husband for forty-one years She resides in Queens Village New York.

As a young girl growing up she states. She loved to read and write and would devour any book she could get her hands on. She would sometime make up her own stories and felt they were better than the books she read.

She is the founder of Cats Theatre Ministry a theatre group founded in 2005. And have written several plays. "God Is Punishing Me" "I found My Husband" "When is Enough Enough" "Waiting on the Lord" and "The Blood". Her plays have been performed in New York and Virginia.

Beside The Perfect Relationship, her second book "The Strictness of Mama" should be out hopefully next Year.

Dr. Brown states "She is passionate about the word of God and its power to transform lives and will forever be thankful to Our

Lord and Savior Jesus Christ for the gift of writing he had given to me."

"Continual Thanks and Praise to God shall always be on my lips",

24992247R00134

Made in the USA
Columbia, SC
31 August 2018